HIS MOMENT TO STEAL

CATHRYN FOX

ISBN 978-1-928056-58-4
Print ISBN 978-1-928056-75-1

1

Jesus, those had to be the biggest melons he'd ever set eyes on.

Security expert Luke Phillips swallowed down the saliva pooling on his tongue and stared at the gorgeous woman coming his way. With his mouth watering for a taste of those juicy, oversized melons, his gaze traveled upward to meet with a set of big blue eyes that held a measure of panic.

"Shit," he mumbled, and discarded his cart to help. It wasn't like he'd actually planned on purchasing any of the groceries inside, anyway. No, like any good thief, he was simply pretending to be a customer when all the while he was actually scoping out the place. Seconds before the woman's armload of honeydews went crashing to the floor, Luke quickly closed the distance between them and reached out to help her.

"Here, let me lighten your load." His cock twitched. Okay, wrong choice of words...

She stopped dead in her tracks, her dark lashes blinking rapidly in confusion as she stared up at him. His head came back with a start, surprised by her reaction. What, had she never been offered help before?

"It's okay, I got it." She arched her back as she awkwardly shifted the gigantic fruits before they fell and splattered on the polished tile floor.

Ignoring her protest, he grabbed three melons, leaving her with two, and glanced at the nametag pinned to her apron. *Emery*. Different, but pretty. Like her.

"Now what kind of guy would I be if I just stood here watching you juggle your melons?" He tossed her his best flirtatious grin trying to make light of the situation and put a smile on her face.

"Thanks," she mumbled, but instead of playing along, she gestured with a nod to the table set up at the end of the grocery aisle. *Tough crowd.* "You can put them there. But just so you know, I did have everything under control." She jutted her chin out a little bit, and Luke's grin widened as she tried to hold her own against him.

"Are you always this stubborn?" He took in the curves her work apron did little to hide. Stubborn, yet sexy. Damned if she wasn't his kind of girl.

She shook her head and loose blonde curls flared around her shoulders. He breathed in the floral fragrance of her shampoo, pulling it deep into his lungs as it overshadowed the scent of ripe honeydew.

"I'm not... I just... Look, I'm just in a hurry, that's all." She placed the melons on the table, adjusted the sale sign, then glanced at her watch. "I have to be somewhere in ten minutes."

He took in the worry in her eyes and the pink tinge on her cheeks before he stole a peek at his own watch. At twelve noon he too had to be somewhere. Not that he had far to go. No, his meeting was with the owner of the upscale market smack dab in the middle of Austin's trendiest neighborhood

—a market he never, ever thought he'd step foot in again. If it weren't for the youth who hung out at Sheffield Community Center, he'd have stayed as far away from the place as possible. But he'd promised the kids new equipment and since he never went back on his word, he had no choice but to take the job. That, and the owner was now a woman, which had him thinking Taylor's Market had changed hands in the last decade. Yeah, he was pretty certain the man who fought to put the "kid from the wrong side of the tracks" in juvenile detention—and won—had retired and was long gone from the place.

"I'm no efficiency expert, but more hands make lighter work." He followed her back to the pile of melons she was moving, and assuming she had to rush off to some appointment on her lunch break, he added, "Shouldn't you get one of the other staff members to help if you have to be out of here in ten?"

Something troubled passed over her pretty eyes as she grabbed another armload and shifted them in the crook of her elbow. She pinched her lips tight, then said, "We're short staffed."

Of course they were, which was probably why the owner, Mrs. Vincent, had called his company looking for a security expert in the first place. Overworked staff had a negative impact on employee health, leading to shortages due to stress-related illnesses. It also had a negative impact on the business itself. With no one watching the store, a thief could easily rob Taylor's Market blind—and likely had—considering they were looking for his services.

Luke had come to the market early to get a feel for their security, and as he stole another glance around, he could see why they needed his help. The place was packed with customers, and there were only three employees on the floor: Emery working produce, a young man behind the deli counter, and one cashier working the front register. Unfortunately, there was no management to be found. Not that Luke thought management would ever help a lowly employee. God forbid anyone in the upper echelons get their hands dirty.

Or give second chances...

But they should at least be watching the store and monitoring the place for theft.

He helped her carry another armload, finishing off the stack, and took note of a young boy around fourteen years old combing the aisles. From the way his T-shirt jutted out from his baggy jeans, it was easy to tell the kid had a pocketful of stolen goods. Luke exhaled slowly, memories of his own youth bombarding him as he kept watchful eyes on the little delinquent. The kid glanced at him, made eye contact, then moved to the next aisle.

Even though Luke wasn't officially on the job yet, he placed the last of the melons on the display table, knowing he had to do something. Stepping into soldier mode he excused himself and walked to the front of the store. He had every intention of catching up with her later to get her number.

He stood by the door and once again took in all the holes in the store's security system as he waited for the kid to exit. Even though it was nearing his appointment time, he wanted to deal with the boy first. At least if he was the one doling out the punishment the kid stood half a chance. Painful past experiences had taught him that the rich lived by their own rules and were biased against those outside their elite circle.

When he saw the boy round an aisle and sidestep the long line at the cash register, Luke picked up a box of specialty cookies and pretended to study the ingredients, giving the boy a chance to escape. For his plan to work, he needed to catch the kid red-handed, outside the store.

The boy slipped out the door. Luke put the box down and followed. He walked behind him for a few seconds, moisture breaking out on his forehead as the warm sunshine heated the sidewalk and radiated upward.

He closed the gap, and when he was within arm's reach he said, "Hey."

The boy spun around, and his eyes went wide with recognition as Luke glared at him. "What the fuck do you want, man?"

Nice...

Luke gestured with a nod. "How about everything in your pockets."

"Shit." The kid cursed and turned to run. Since Luke had anticipated the boy's next move he was already one step ahead of him and had him by the scruff before he could round the corner and bolt.

Luke turned him around and nudged him toward the market, hoping to find a quiet place inside. "How about we have a little talk?"

"How about you go fuck yourself."

"That's a nice mouth you've got there," Luke said. "Do you kiss your mother good night with it?"

"I kiss lots of girls with it." He smirked and struggled against Luke's grip, but this wasn't Luke's first rodeo. In fact, a little over a decade ago, many of his friends had stood where the boy was right now—and Luke had spent three years in juvenile detention because of it.

Luke practically dragged him inside and when he found a handful of customers staring at him, he searched for Emery. The commotion must have caught her attention. She rushed from the back of the store and when she saw him with the struggling boy, her eyes went wide.

"Is there an office around here I can use for a minute?" Luke asked.

"What's going on?"

"What's going on is this kid has a pocket full of goods."

"Oh, I didn't..." When she pushed her curls from her face, Luke noticed a worried frown creasing her forehead. She pointed toward the back. "I was busy. I didn't see."

"It's fine. I've got it under control," Luke explained, not wanting her to think the blame was hers. It was management's job to train the staff and put theft prevention measures in place.

"Are you a cop?" she asked.

"Something like that." The kid elbowed Luke in the gut and Luke tensed. "About that room," he said between gritted teeth.

She nodded and he followed her to the back of the store. She pulled a ring full of keys from her pocket and unlocked the door with shaky fingers. Luke stepped past her and she followed him. Once inside the small office, Luke shoved the kid into a chair and leaned against the desk, taking an authoritative, high-powered position over him, a tactic he'd learned in the army. Emery stood by the door, looking completely unsure of herself—of Luke—and the situation she'd suddenly found herself in. Luke could have told her to leave, but he needed her there for two reasons. One, she would be a witness to what he was about to do, and two, he was a selfish prick and liked being around her. And of course, he couldn't forget that he'd yet to get her number.

"What's your name?" Luke asked the boy, lowering his voice slightly.

"Captain America," the kid responded with a smirk.

Luke let that statement stand for a while as he assessed the boy. One thing was for sure, he wasn't as tough as he wanted Luke to think he was. He took in his ratty shirt, jeans that were two sizes too big, and sneakers that had seen better days. As the puzzle known as Captain America clicked together, Luke felt his heart pinch, but he kept his face hard, his voice deep.

"So what are you, some kind of street thug?"

The kid slouched in his chair, his nonchalant body language belying the worry backlighting his dark eyes. As a former military security specialist, Luke knew all about reading people, and despite trying to appear unfazed, the kid was scared shitless. Which meant Luke had him right where he wanted him. If the kid really was a badass, there was no way Luke could get him to agree to the terms he was about to lay out.

Captain American folded his arms—a protective measure to shield himself, and a sure sign of his anxiety. "Yeah, that's what I am," he answered. "A street thug with superpowers."

Luke gave him his best hard-assed glare and stared at him for longer than was comfortable. Eventually the boy shifted, straightening slightly in his seat. Good. At least somewhere deep inside he still held a degree of respect for authority and wasn't a lost cause.

Luke met his gaze unflinchingly. "Did someone put you up to this?"

After a long moment, the boy tore his gaze away and stared at his sneakers, ending the uncomfortable stare down. "Here, just take the stuff." He reached into his pocket and pulled out two pieces of red licorice and tossed them onto the desk.

"You don't seem like a stupid kid." Luke picked up the candy and slapped it against his palm. Behind the boy's nervousness he had a solid determination about him, an intelligence that ran deep. "In fact, I'd say you're pretty smart, which makes me wonder why you're willing to ruin your life for two pieces of licorice."

"I'm not... I didn't... I don't..." He pushed agitated fingers through dark, shoulder-length hair that looked like it hadn't been shampooed in weeks.

"This can go down one of two ways," Luke began. "I call

in backup and you end up in juvie for stealing…" He paused to give the kid a moment to chew on that, even though he had no intention of ever calling the cops.

"Fuck," the boy mumbled, his voice cracking slightly. "Look, the licorice wasn't even for me."

"So someone did put you up to this."

He stared at the floor, and fisted his hair. "It's for my little brother, okay? He likes licorice."

"Your little brother?"

"Yeah, he's only three and doesn't get…" He stopped talking, like he didn't want to give away too much.

"What else do you have in your pockets?" The boy hesitated, and Luke reached for the phone.

"Okay, fine." He pulled out a tube of deli meats and slapped it on the table.

Luke picked up the package and exchanged a look with Emery. Troubled eyes full of mixed emotions stared back, a clear sign that she knew what was going on. Taylor's Market might have been in Austin's trendiest neighborhood, but just a few blocks away things went south fast. Luke knew first-hand what it was like to live in the city's poverty district, where food and candy were hard to come by.

"Is this for your brother too?" he asked, keeping his face hard. A kid like Captain America here would never want his pity.

"Yeah." He emptied his other pocket and placed a couple of crusty rolls on the desk. "So what's the other way?"

"The other way?" Luke asked.

"You said this could go down one of two ways."

"The other way is you spend every weekend this summer at the community center out in Sheffield."

"Fuck. Isn't that where old people hang out?"

Old people, young people, therapy dogs. Luke picked the phone up.

"Don't. I'll do it," the boy said. Luke continued to glare at him, waiting for a stronger reaction. The boy cursed under his breath, held his hands up, palms out. "I'll do it, okay. Just put the damn phone down."

Luke took his hand off the receiver. "Get up, kid."

The boy stood. "It's Trent, and I'm not a kid."

"Okay, Trent," he began, giving him that much, despite the fact that he *was* a kid—one who not only needed, but was craving guidance in the worst way. "Where do you live?"

He narrowed suspicious eyes. "Why?"

"Because I'm going to walk you home so I'll know where to find you if you don't show up on Saturday."

"Fine," he mumbled.

After he gave the address, Luke nudged him toward the door, but didn't miss Emery jotting the address down on a whiteboard hung near the desk. For a moment he thought she might report him, but he'd seen the look in her eyes. She felt for the kid every bit as much as Luke did. "And don't think you're getting off easy. Juvie might look like a day in the park after a weekend at the center."

He moved to the door and the sweet floral scent of Emery hit him as she stood there nibbling her bottom lip, looking at him with an equal mixture of worry and relief. "Listen, will you tell the owner that I'll be late for my appointment?"

As if a light bulb had just gone off, her big eyes went wide. She shook her head, her long curls bouncing around her shoulders. "You're...you're Mr. Phillips...from..." Her words fell off and she finished with, "I should have known."

He stopped dead in his tracks and took a moment to look at her. She really was gorgeous, but there was something in her eyes that told him she wore the weight of the world on her shoulders. Damned if he didn't want to help lighten that load too.

"Yeah. I'm Luke Phillips, from Phillips Security." He gave

her a suggestive smile, along with a teasing wink, determined to loosen her up and put a smile on that lush mouth of hers. He pitched his voice low, for her ears only and said, "Which means I'll be hanging out here for the next few weeks and while I'm here, you'll never again have to juggle your melons alone."

Emery Vincent tried to quiet her racing heart as she watched Mr. Phillips, or rather Luke-o-licious, escort the boy from her office. Surprised that her legs could actually move, she crossed the small tile floor and plopped herself down in her old leather chair, her mind racing with this unexpected turn of events. When she'd called Phillips Security and talked to his receptionist, she expected a hardened soldier to show up, not sex in a formfitting T-shirt.

You'll never again have to juggle your melons alone.

Oh, God!

He'd been teasing her, flirting with her, but she'd been too focused on her upcoming meeting—on losing the business her ailing father had left her in hands—to partake in his sexy banter.

Unable to help herself she stole a glance at him as he walked down the deli aisle with delinquent Trent in tow. As she thanked her lucky stars that he was good at his job and had stopped one more theft, she took in his long, hard legs and low-slung jeans that cradled his backside to perfection— and oh what a backside it was.

After a good, long look, her gaze traveled up to take in a wide back and even wider shoulders. She caught a glimpse of his tattoo peeking out from the short sleeves of his T-shirt, and her fingers itched to explore the rest of him to see if he had any more ink. She continued to stare, unable to help herself, but when he turned back and caught her ogling, he gave her a sexy, lopsided smile—one that spoke of hot nights and even hotter sex.

Oh my...

Okay, so she totally knew what his teasing was all about. The man wanted her between the sheets. Hell, who was she kidding? She wanted that too. The last time she'd crawled into bed with a guy was a little over two years ago. That lust-affair hadn't ended well. Then again, for as long as she could remember, none of her relationships ever had. In kinder-garten no one wanted to play with the girl who had a "retarded" brother, as they called him, because they thought it might rub off. God, kids were so damn cruel, twisting that clinical word to make it so ugly and offensive when all it really meant was that he had special needs. It was wrong to call people names, any kind of name. Simple as that.

In Emery's later years, kids started talking to her when they found out her folks ran the market. They befriended her, only to score free candy and soda in their middle school years, and alcohol and smokes in their later ones—which she ended up paying for.

She'd learned the hard way that people hung out with her for one reason and one reason only—they wanted something. And that something was never a lifelong friendship, or a lasting romantic love affair, like she really wanted.

From his outwardly flirtatious personality, she assumed Luke was a player, which was fine by her. She wasn't opposed to a night of sex with a hot guy like him—no strings attached. Hey, at least her eyes were wide open and she knew never to trust, never to set herself up for failure. And, hell, a night in the sack would undoubtedly help ease the tension that had been building inside her since taking over the business two years ago—and watching it go downhill. Things had been good for the first year, but then over the last twelve months she started losing thousands of dollars every pay period. With an expanding neighborhood, and a busier store, she chalked the losses up to theft, but lack of cash flow meant she had to lay off employees. Less staff meant fewer people to watch the store, which only compounded the problem.

She exhaled slowly, her mind going back to Luke and the reason she'd called his company in the first place. From his teasing banter she guessed he had no idea she was the owner of the market. She'd always gone by Vincent-Taylor and had dropped the Taylor from her last name a few years ago, keeping her mother's name only. Partly to honor her after she died, and partly because, well, everyone wanted something from a Taylor. Her father had numerous connections in high places, and many favors were traded. Emery just wanted people to like her for who she was, not for what she could give them—or do for them.

Regardless, now was not the time to be thinking about that, not when her father had trusted her with the business and she needed to make it a success not only for him, but also for her older brother. The residential health facility where he received around-the-clock nursing care was expensive, but it was also the best facility in the state, and she wasn't about to jeopardize his well-being due to lack of funds. He was counting on her and she wouldn't let him down, which meant all her focus had to go into saving the market.

She took a crisp twenty-dollar bill from her purse and jotted Trent's address down on a sticky note. Pushing to her feet, she made her way into the market with the product Luke had left on her desk.

Luke...

Hot, hard, so nice to look at. She thought about the way he'd shifted gears with Trent, and in seconds flat had gone from flirtatious to deadly serious. She'd caught the intense glint in his steel-gray eyes as he hardened himself, and suspected there was more to him than met the eye. Beneath all the charm and charisma she suspected that ex-soldier Luke Phillips had a past that continued to haunt him. Behind the charming grin, and flirty smile, there was a darker part of him.

Even still, her body was screaming at her to cut loose and have some much-needed fun with the guy who oozed sex. But she had a business to fix, she reminded herself. Which meant she needed to concentrate on running the market, and not on what her body craved.

Then again, look how that had turned out for her.

Yeah, some inner voice yelled—probably the one calling the shots from between her legs—*look where that got you. Go ahead, have some fun with Luke-o-licious. Let him juggle your melons. You know you want to.*

②

Luke drove his hands into his pockets and leaned against the doorjamb, his gaze raking over sweet yet sexy Emery as she sat at the same desk where he'd recently interrogated Trent. She was so focused on the sheet of paper in front of her that she hadn't noticed him watching. It was nearing twelve thirty and he wondered what she was still doing here. Didn't she have to be somewhere?

Wait…was she? Nah, she couldn't be. Could she?

Shit.

"Oh," she said, her cheeks turning a pretty shade of pink as she glanced up at him. "I didn't realize you were back."

He angled his head, an uneasy feeling searing his gut as he looked at her ring finger. Even though it was empty, he said, "Mrs. Vincent, right?"

"Miss Vincent," she corrected.

Christ, how could he have missed it? Probably because he'd been too busy flirting with her to realize *why* she had the weight of the world on her shoulders. This was her business—her upscale market—which meant that technically she was his boss.

What the hell was it he'd said about her melons?

Never mind that, he'd been lusting after her and she was one of *them*. Rich, elite, never one to give second chances. Anger moved through him and he wondered if he'd read her wrong earlier where Trent was concerned. Maybe she'd taken his address down because she planned on turning him in.

"Now that you've seen firsthand on what's going on here..." she paused and seemed a bit breathless as she gestured toward the chair on the other side of her desk, "...I guess you know why I called your company?"

With his defenses in place, he hardened himself and sat across from her. "Are you going turn him in?"

Her brow furrowed, and the pink tinge on her cheeks spread. "Why would I do that?"

"Why did you take down his information?"

She blinked rapidly and looked at the white board. "I...I...just."

"What the hell?" A sharp voice boomed from the doorway.

Luke turned to see Winston Taylor glaring at him, as in Winston Taylor, the man who used to own Taylor's Market and had connections in very high places. Well fuck if his day didn't just go from bad to worse. He gripped the arms of his chair hard enough to break them, and even though he was no longer in the army, every muscle in his body tensed, ready for battle.

Emery stood up. "Dad, what's going on?"

Dad?

Her father jerked his head toward Luke, his gaze razor sharp. "What's going on?" he spouted, spittle flying from his mouth. "I could be asking you the same question."

Emery cast a confused look Luke's way, then turned back to her father.

In that moment, Luke's mind raced back to a little over

twelve years ago. He vaguely remembered hearing that the man who wanted to crucify him had a daughter around Luke's age. Not that they ran in the same circles or went to the same schools. They didn't. Even though she went by a different last name, it should have occurred to him that Taylor would have handed the business down to his offspring after his wife had died—yeah, Luke remembered hearing about her death just before he was put away.

"You're not making any sense," Emery said.

Her father scowled, his eyes full of hate as he glared at Luke. He pointed his cane Luke's way. "Do you have any idea who that...that is?" he spat out, like he couldn't bring himself to voice Luke's name.

"Luke Phillips," she said. "I hired his company to set up a new security system for the store."

"Security system?" He narrowed his eyes suspiciously and spun back toward Emery. "What's wrong with our old one?"

"Insurance purposes." She gave an easy shrug, the fib rolling off her tongue like she'd spent hours practicing it. "Changes in the policy, that's all."

Luke angled his head, curious about her lie, but said nothing.

The old man waved a dismissive hand in Luke's direction. "So you hired him?" With that he laughed out loud. Not a humorous kind of laugh, more like a cynical one. "Well I guess it takes one to know one."

Emery shook her head as Luke climbed to his feet. Okay, enough of this. He wasn't a frightened sixteen-year-old boy anymore, and very little scared or intimated him these days. Juvie did that to a guy. So did the army.

He glared at the man who'd taken so much from him—his father, his sister, his teenage years. "What he's trying to say," Luke began, "is that I'm the guy he put away for stealing."

"That's right," Taylor said. He jutted his chest out, and if he didn't look so old, so pathetic, Luke might have considered clocking him. "Someone had to teach you and the rest of those hooligans you ran with that you just couldn't walk in here and take what you wanted without consequences."

Emery's eyes widened, but Luke just stood there, the things he felt for this man burning a hole in his gut. There was no point in telling Emery the truth. That he wasn't the one who'd taken a loaf of crusty bread and a jar of peanut butter to feed a pregnant girlfriend. Or that he'd taken the fall for his buddy because unlike Luke, Shane was of legal age and there was no way in hell he'd have made it in jail. Yeah, stealing was wrong. Luke knew that. His father was a religious man and had drilled that into him and his sister when they were young. But sometimes desperation drove a guy to do desperate things. He could tell her all that but why bother?

Few people believed him—believed in him—so why would she?

"Don't hire him, Emery. Once a thief always a thief and nothing good can come from this," Taylor said.

Luke glared at the man as Emery's head bobbed back and forth between the two, like she had no idea what to do next. Financially, Luke needed this job, but he wasn't about to stand here and take any more shit from the Taylor family. Nor was he going to come between a daughter and her father. Not ever again. It wasn't that he thought father knew best. He didn't. But a girl needed her dad, especially when she didn't have a mother. Of that he was certain, and it was the reason he hadn't spoken to his kid sister in over twelve years.

With that last thought in mind, he took a step toward the door, figuring he'd somehow find another way to support the community center. Maybe he'd even dip into his savings. Expanding his business could wait a little longer, although he'd been hoping to give a few of his army buddies a steady paycheck when they discharged next month.

Luke clamped his hands behind his neck, ready to walk away from the contract. He'd never quit a job before. He'd never quit at anything. But in this case he didn't expect he'd have to. He fully expected Emery to fire him on the spot after finding out about his past. But what she said next not only surprised him, it shocked him to his core.

"Well that was a long time ago."

"You have got to be kidding me," her father said, practically frothing at the mouth as he banged his cane on the floor.

There was a real sadness on Emery's face, a deep worry in her eyes as she sat back down in her chair, indicating that Luke do the same. Mumbling curses under his breath, her father stormed off, cracking his cane hard against the floor.

"I'm open to hearing all your ideas," she said. "After what happened here earlier, I'm sure you can see that I really need help."

He looked over her face, assessing her, and as she gave him an almost pleading look, something inside him gave, softened. He wasn't sure what it was about her, and even though she was one of *them*, he found himself wanting to help her, wanting to protect her. He could tell she was strong, had been strong for a long time, and wasn't the kind of girl to ask for help. But she was asking him right now.

He listened to her talk, and when she placed a paper in front of him, the layout of the store, he scanned it.

Emery looked at him. "My father," she began. "He doesn't usually come around too much anymore. His health, it's failing."

"Emery..." he said even though he had no idea what it was he wanted to say to her.

Walk away, Luke. Just walk away.

He glanced at the store's layout again, then looked into her big hopeful eyes. When he opened his mouth, to tell her he couldn't take the job, he suddenly found himself saying, "We have a lot of work to do."

Shit.

He thought he caught a flicker of a smile on her face before she switched into full business mode. "Okay, what's our first order of business?"

"First I'd like to hang around the store to observe, then I'd like to set up surveillance cameras and get my team to watch from the monitors in my truck. Once I see the thieves in action, I'll know where we have to make changes in the layout, cameras, et cetera."

She nodded, and once again the smell of her sweet floral shampoo reached his nostrils. His fingers curled around the arms of the chair as his cock shifted.

Easy, boy. She's not the one for you.

"I'll give you a rundown of the store and then let you and your team get to work." She climbed from her seat. "If you have any questions or need anything, you know where to find me."

Luke followed her into the market, and after a tour, he spent the rest of the afternoon pretending to shop so he could observe the flow of customers and the areas that were cut off from view. By the time night rolled around, he hopped onto his motorcycle and made his way to the bar, in need of a drink, and maybe a fist to the face from one of his comrades. Yeah, perhaps a punch to the head would knock some sense back into him. What the hell was he thinking agreeing to stay on?

He pushed his way through the heavy front door and plunked himself down next to his buddy, Garrett Andersen. "Hey," he said to the former military security specialist turned city cop.

After a long moment Garrett nudged him with his elbow. "What the hell is the matter with you?"

Twisting restlessly on his stool at Sky Bar, his favorite after work hangout, Luke looked up from the beer he was nursing and said, "Nothing, just thinking about the new job I just contracted."

"Oh yeah, is she hot?"

Luke laughed. "Fuck off."

"Is who hot?" Matt James asked as he came through the back door and took the empty seat beside Luke at the end of bar. He unzipped his backpack and slapped his books onto the bar top.

"The girl at the new job site," Garrett provided.

"Ah," Matt said. "So that's why you're all mopey?"

"Mopey? Christ, Matt. You sound like your grandmother."

Matt shrugged, reached back into his bag and pulled out a jar of peanut butter and a plastic spoon.

Luke shook his head. For as long as he'd known Matt, the guy had been eating peanut butter from a jar. At least he'd upgraded to a spoon than from his damn finger. "You know you're not twelve anymore, right?"

"I'm a poor college kid now," Matt said. "I just got out of class so I eat what I can, when I can."

Just then, Sky, the owner of the bar, came sauntering over. "Then eat this." She slid a whole-wheat ham and cheese sandwich, along with a garden salad, in front of Matt.

The smile that lit up Matt's face damn near blinded Luke, and made him wonder why his friend had never made a move on Sky. They all went way back—Caleb and Shane making up the fourth and fifth members of their group—and Matt lit up like a kid on Christmas morning whenever she was around. After Matt, Caleb, Shane and Luke had returned from overseas, and Matt enrolled in college, Sky gave him a job at the bar, allowing him to work around his classes. The two were tight, but Luke had the feeling that Sky had something for Caleb—who was down in San Antonio working in the medical clinic.

Despite the sandwich, Matt opened the jar of peanut butter and stuck in the spoon. He held it out to Luke. "Want some?"

"Get that shit away from me." Luke shoved Matt's arm. "You know I'm allergic."

Matt laughed, and flipped open his MCAT book. "Yeah, but I thought it would be good to see firsthand what an allergic swelling looks like. You know, in case it's on the test."

"Piss off, Matt." Luke offered him his best hard-assed face, and made a fist. "Or I'll teach you a thing or two about swelling."

Matt grinned and turned his attention to his sandwich and thick book. Garrett asked Sky to bring two more beers. After she delivered them, he turned to Luke.

"So who is she?" he asked, keeping his voice low since Matt was studying beside them.

"Don't you have a pretty wife and little girl waiting for you at home?" he asked, not wanting to talk about Emery or how curious he was about her. *Why did she lie to her father? Why did she still hire him for security, of all things, after finding out about his past?*

"Hey, don't be jealous, man," Garrett teased.

Luke laughed. "Me? Jealous? No way." He looked at the cute blonde who had just sauntered in the door. "I'm good right where I am." Truthfully, it wasn't that he was opposed to marriage, but he enjoyed dating different women. He wasn't a man whore, but he liked variety. Nothing wrong with that as far as he was concerned. Maybe someday when he found the right one he'd consider settling down. Although he was pretty sure he wasn't going to find his soul mate at Sky Bar. Most of the singles that came there were simply looking for a good time.

"Okay, so tell me about this job," Garrett said, all teasing gone from his voice. "What's the name of the company, and why do you look like you're standing on the front line about to take a direct hit from the enemy?"

"Because I am." Luke looked at his friend, his comrade. As a fellow army security specialist, he'd worked closely with Garrett in the field. And even though Garrett had demons, and had learned to overcome them thanks to Tallulah, he was a guy Luke trusted with his life. They spent many nights talking in the field, and Garrett was one of a handful of guys who knew about his past.

"Go on."

Luke twisted off his beer cap, took a long pull from the bottle and set it down. He let loose a breath, gave a hard shake of his head, and said, "You wouldn't believe it if I told you."

"Try me."

He met Garrett's glance. "Taylor's Market."

Garrett planted his elbows on the table, and blew out a slow breath. "What the hell were you thinking? Wait, let me guess..." He paused and smacked Luke on the side of the head. "You weren't thinking with this."

"I thought the owners had changed over the years, then I found out it was Taylor's daughter Emery running the show."

"You could have walked away."

"I could have. But I need all the work I can get," he said, although deep in his gut he knew Emery was the reason... Emery with the big pleading eyes...

Garrett nodded, because he knew Luke was financially tapped, every spare cent he made going into the scholarship fund. "How is Allison?"

His heart tightened at the mention of his sister. He drew

a breath and let it out slowly. "She's good. She graduated the top of her class and is now in law school."

"Law school, huh?" Garrett twirled his beer bottle on the tabletop. "Maybe she wants to right some wrongs."

"Hopefully," Luke said.

"She still doesn't know."

"Of course not. The scholarship fund was set up anonymously for a reason. If she knew it came from me she wouldn't take it." He looked into his beer bottle, his stomach in knots. He might not have talked to his sister in ages, but he still kept close tabs on her. "She hates me, Garrett."

"You did what you had to do, Luke. I get that. And I bet she doesn't hate you." He took a sip of beer and went quiet for a moment, like he was deep in thought. "Maybe you should try talking to her."

"Yeah, maybe," he said, and even though he knew Garrett was right—he had to do what he had to do—it didn't make pushing his sister away from him, or turning her against him any easier. But he couldn't let their father turn his back on her too, all because she wanted to visit her big brother in juvie.

The old man was disgusted with Luke after the incident and wanted nothing more to do with him. Nor did he want Allison visiting or having any connection with a Phillips who would shame his entire family. The bastard had given Luke an ultimatum—either he put Allison out of his life and stopped her from visiting or the old man would disown her as well. Luke had no choice but to push her away—for her own good.

When Luke took the blame he never thought Taylor's connections ran deep and he'd end up in juvie. Community service yes, but never locked in a hellhole where he was forced to use his fists more than once to survive. Another kick to the teeth was that Dear Old Dad had turned against him. He sure found out who had his back—and more importantly who didn't—when he found himself in trouble. His father had died a few years ago, never knowing the truth, because he refused to speak to his only son, deeming him unworthy. Jesus, they'd all lost so much.

"So speaking of doing what you have to do, what are you going to do about Taylor's daughter?"

"I don't know."

"You like her?"

"I did before I found out who she was."

"And now you don't like her."

"Yeah, no, I don't know." Okay, now he sounded like Trent.

"I messed in the wrong sandbox once," Garrett said, grinning. He held his hand up to show off his wedding ring. "And look how that turned out."

"Didn't you get your ass kicked by Ving over that?"

"Yeah, but it was worth it. I married the sweetest girl in the world and she gave me a beautiful daughter."

"I wanted to sleep with Emery, not marry her," Luke said.

"Yeah, that's what I thought about Tallulah too."

Luke scoffed. "Whose side are you on here anyway?"

"Come on." Garrett nudged him with his elbow. "You know I've got your back."

"Then maybe you should try to give advice that's actually useful."

Garrett laughed, then glanced at his watch and stood. "How about this. If you want to get her out of your head—" he paused and gestured toward the cute blonde girl who was casting glances Luke's way, "—she's just the girl to help." Garrett dropped a few bills on the bar, then put his hand on Luke's shoulder. "But you know, it wasn't her that did wrong by you."

"Ah, about that *good* advice..."

Garrett twirled the ring on his finger. "Look, all I'm saying is you never know what you can *build* when playing with someone else's sand."

He wasn't looking to *build* anything with Emery. "It wasn't her sand I wanted to play with, Garrett. Now go home to your girls and stop pissing me off with your fucked-up analogies. You're starting to sound like Jack."

"And how could that be a bad thing?" Jack Barnes asked as he took over Garrett's seat.

As Garrett laughed and headed for the door, his buddy Jack ordered a drink. Jack was the guy who'd called in a few favors and managed to open the old military base on the outskirts of town where they all trained service dogs.

"So what was Garrett talking to you about?"

"Her," Luke said as he turned his attention to the blonde. Yeah, maybe he would take her home. Maybe she was just the girl to help him get Emery out of his head.

Sweet and sexy, yet strong and stubborn Emery.

Emery who needed him.

Shit.

③

Emery restocked the dry goods section but kept dropping the very expensive boxes of imported crackers because she couldn't quite seem to concentrate. Her glance kept straying to the front of the store in search of Luke, who'd been coming and going all morning with his equipment.

And oh what fine equipment he had...

Honestly, she still couldn't believe she'd gone ahead and hired him after finding out he was the man who'd sent her father on a rampage a little over a decade ago. Even though he'd kept her sheltered from the event, she did remember his rage and how he set out to make an example of the boy. She had no idea what Luke had stolen, but the fact that the courts had sent him to juvie for it, must have meant he'd taken one heck of a big haul.

She was still a little surprised that Luke had agreed to the job after his run-in with her father. She didn't miss the angry flare lingering in the depths of his silvery gaze when he saw him standing in the doorway, when he realized *who* Emery was. Even still, she was glad he'd signed on, and the least she could do was believe that he'd learned his lesson. Truthfully, she didn't trust him on a personal level; then again she didn't trust anyone. But she could only hope that on a professional level he wasn't going to do anything to jeopardize his business and find himself on the wrong side of the law again.

Once a thief always a thief…

As her father's words pinged around her brain, she considered his reaction when he saw Luke sitting across from her. Emery had never gone against her father's wishes before. Everything she did was to keep peace and make him happy—which was why she kept the state of the business to herself. After her mom had died in her early teen years, Jeremy had grown increasingly aggressive, making it difficult for her dad to take care of him. Emery tried to be the quiet one, keeping her grades up and walking around unseen so she didn't give her father any more stress than he already had.

Keeping him happy was important to her, which made her wonder why she hadn't followed his wishes and sent Luke packing. But she already knew the answer to that question. If she didn't hire Luke, what chance did she stand at turning her business around? He was the only game in town, unless she wanted to wait months, which she didn't. Months could be too late for her. But the truth was after seeing him in action with Trent, she felt a little lighter knowing he was good at his job.

She caught a glimpse of him moving through the doorway, a box full of motion-sensing cameras in his arms—hard, strong arms that brushed hers two days ago when he'd helped her with her melons. *Melons…* Emery bit back a groan as she remembered his teasing, as well as the hungry way he looked at her.

But ever since he found out she was Winston Taylor's daughter, that hunger had turned to anger. He now walked around with every muscle tense, his features harsh, his gray eyes cold and calculating as he focused solely on the task at hand. Which was probably a good thing, because honestly, the last thing she should have been doing was having an affair with the man who stole from her father. With him ignoring her, regarding her with dark, haunted eyes, she could keep her mind on her business, where it belonged.

Heavy footsteps heralded someone's approach. She glanced up and came face to face, or rather face to crotch with Luke. Oh God.

What was that I'd just thought about keeping my mind on my business?

She sucked in a quick breath, and when she caught the spicy scent of his skin, she swallowed the moan rising in her throat. Heat zipped through her body, despite the cold air blowing down on her, and she could feel her pale cheeks coloring, her blood burning hotter.

"Are you okay?" Luke asked, his gaze narrowing as he looked at her with steel-gray eyes.

"Yes." She fanned her face. "It's hot in here."

He wiped his brow, his T-shirt stretching tight across his broad shoulders. "It's worse out there."

As she remained on her knees in front of him, Luke lowered his head, his ghostly stare locked on hers. The air went still as he stared at her, his haunting eyes penetrating, looking at her in a way no one else ever had. His eyes seemed to change color, taking on a darker shade of pewter as he raked his fingers through his short hair. Thick muscles flexed and in that instant, sexual heat flooded her, once again reminding her it had been two years since she felt a man touch her body.

Unable to help herself, she moved her gaze to Luke's big hands. She took in his calluses and wondered how they would feel scraping across her skin, touching her in her most intimate of places. This time there was nothing she could do to stifle the moan rumbling in her throat. She grabbed the box of crackers and gave them a little shake to smother her sexually frustrated groan.

The sound seemed to do something to Luke. His head snapped up and he shook it like he was trying to clear it. "Can you come out to the van with me?"

"Oh, yeah, sure," she said, thankful for the distraction. She grabbed the shelf, about to hoist herself up, when his hand closed over hers and tugged. With little effort he pulled her to her feet, and because the movement caught her off guard, she fell against him. His arm snaked around her back, his big fingers splaying over her shirt. Her mind took that moment to wander, visualizing his big, strong body over hers, his lips on her mouth, her breasts, between her legs.

She stood there breathless, his closeness completely overwhelming her. He dipped his head, and their eyes met. "You... ah, you okay?" he asked. "You seem distracted."

Since her voice had just taken a vacation, she nodded, and her hair fell into her face. Luke reached out, like he was about to move it, but then suddenly pulled his hand back like it had been slapped. Just then she could hear the squeaky wheel of a cart coming her way. She smoothed her hands over her apron and skirt, quickly pulling herself together.

"So you needed me at the van."

Luke stiffened and stepped back, the muscles along his jaw clenching as he frowned. "Yeah. I have some things I want to go over with you."

She waved her hand and tried her best to keep her voice light. "Then, please, lead the way."

She followed him out to his van where his crew was working, and a blast of stale heat hit her when she entered. Good God, if she thought it was hot in the store, it was nothing compared to the heat in the van. It was stifling, even with all the windows open. She noticed the empty water bottles and coffee cups where the surveillance monitors were set up. If they didn't stay hydrated they were likely to pass out.

Luke introduced her to the rest of his team, who were watching the monitors. Colt, a very nice-looking guy who appeared to be in his mid-twenties, turned to her and tipped his Stetson. In his best Texas drawl, he said, "Howdy, Emery."

"Colt," she said. "It's nice to meet you."

Tanner shimmied his chair closer, shoving Colt out of the way as he twisted his ball cap around. Translucent blue eyes met hers. "You're only saying that because you don't know him. He's actually a pain in the ass, and it's never nice to meet him. Now me, however..."

"Hey," Colt said, ramming his chair against Tanner's. "I saw her first."

"You see what I have to put up with?" Luke asked, shaking his head. "It's like herding fucking monkeys."

"I'd rather be a monkey than a hardheaded mule like you," Colt shot back.

"You mean hardheaded ass," Tanner said, laughing.

Emery watched the way the three interacted, loving the easy camaraderie between friends. It was obvious they were all close and cared a great deal about each other. She knew Luke was ex-military and couldn't help but wonder if these two were ex-soldiers as well. As she thought about that and listened to them razz each other, some small part of her heart tightened, wishing she had experienced this kind of friendship growing up. But if past experiences had taught her anything it was to never open up to anyone.

Unable to help herself, she smiled up at Luke, and when she did something in his face softened, making him look so adorable, so sexy and boyish it took two locked knees to keep herself standing. For extra measure, she grabbed the edge of the counter, gripping it like it was a lifeline.

"Are you okay?" Luke asked, slipping his hand around her waist and holding her against him.

As she once again found herself in his arms, the hard-packed muscles on his chest and stomach pressing against her, it was all she could do to fill her lungs. "It's just so warm in here," she fibbed.

"Yeah, it is." He held her longer and his fingers felt hot, heavy against the small of her back. "Here, sit down. Once the equipment arrives, we'll be able to do the monitoring from your office, but for now, this is what we have to work with." He pulled a chair out for her and when she lowered herself he nodded to Tanner. "Grab her some water."

Tanner shook one of the empty bottles. "We're out, man."

Emery held her hands up. "It's okay. I'm okay, really." Before Luke could protest, she turned her attention to the monitors. "Can you tell me what's happening here?" she asked, redirecting the conversation.

Images flashed before her, showing her different angles of the market. Luke leaned over her, and as his hard stomach muscles pressed against her body once again, she had no idea how she was going to concentrate. Good God, the guy was so hard, so hot, so tempting. Too bad he no longer seemed interested in her.

Which was for the best, she reminded herself.

"You see right here?" he said, pointing to different areas of the store as the images flicked by. "And here?"

She nodded, and leaned toward the monitor. "Yeah."

"Blind spots," he said. "We definitely have to add cameras here and here." His finger moved over the glass, and as he traced the screen, she imagined that rough pad of his index finger tracing another area of her body...just like that.

Good God, Emery. Get it together.

With the heat getting to her, not to mention Luke's closeness, she peeled off her apron and set it on her lap. She heard

Luke exhale slowly, his warm breath tickling her neck. She shifted as his presence grew invasive, overwhelming.

"This all sounds good to me," she said.

"Yeah, but there are going to be extra costs involved."

Luke stayed close, too close, and he looked a little restless when she twisted in her chair. Her shoulder rubbed up against his stomach as she mentally went over her budget, and while she couldn't afford it, she couldn't afford not to either. "Okay," she said.

For the next twenty minutes Luke talked to her about security measures, going over things from advanced surveillance software that could compare a shopper's movement between video images and recognize unusual activity, to predicting where a shoplifter was likely to hide. The system also recorded the opening of back doors, and took snapshots of the perpetrator. He then went over the use of RFID—radio frequency identification chips—which could be imbedded in the wheels on each shopping cart, as well as on products, to monitor inventory.

Not only was she fascinated by the information, she was also impressed with his vast knowledge and his passion as he explained it all to her. One thing was for certain, the man was intelligent and truly loved what he did.

When he was done, Colt pulled out a number pad and set it next to one of the monitors.

Luke pointed to it, and that's when she noticed the corkboard behind Tanner. A picture of a girl stood out amongst the dozen or so notes. She looked to be around twenty, and for a moment she wondered who she was, and what she meant to one of these guys, but turned her attention back to Luke when he started talking to her.

"Right now I have to get back inside and work on the electrical, so Colt is going to go over how to set the system once it's in place."

Colt's chair squeaked as he shifted closer, his blue eyes holding a bit of mischief as they raked over her. "So, Emery," he said. "What's your number, sweetheart?" From the look on his face, she knew he wasn't talking about the key code for the number pad he was holding.

"Colt," Luke warned.

Looking a bit sheepish, Colt shot a glance over his shoulder. "What?"

When Emery turned to face Luke he shook his head and said, "Stay away from him. He's trouble."

Emery grinned when she caught a ghost of a smile on Luke's mouth, like he'd forgotten who she was and how much he hated her family.

Unable to help herself she shot back with, "Yeah, well something tells me he'd probably say the same about you."

With that both Colt and Tanner laughed. "She's got you there, boss man," Tanner said.

"Oh, really. So you're going to side with them, are you?" Luke shook his head, the corner of his mouth twitching. "You should have stuck with me, sunshine. Those two will lead you down a path you might not want to go on."

"You're one to talk," Colt shot back.

That ghost of a grin returned. "Yeah, but at least my path would be paved with good intentions."

"Good intentions, my ass," Tanner said.

"Why does everything have to be about your ass?" Luke asked.

Colt laughed. "Because he's got an ass fixation, that's why."

Luke pointed to the keypad, the hint of a smile gone. "Teach Emery how to use that, and keep your hands to yourselves."

With that, Luke slipped out of the van and Emery turned her attention to Colt. Too bad her mind was still on Luke and the way her name rolled off his tongue. She wondered what his voice would sound like during sex, soft and raspy, or harsh and rough.

When Colt started talking, she gave a hard shake of her head to clear it and turned her focus to him. Over the next half hour, she learned the ins and outs of the system Luke had customized for her and how to program her alarm system. Every now and then she'd glance at her monitor and catch Luke at work, his hard body maneuvering around the aisles with stealth and confidence, his every movement dragging her focus with it.

Once she had the system mastered, she made her way back inside the bustling air-conditioned market, passing Luke as he stepped outside, looking hot and tired and in need of a break. She went to her office, where there were no cameras, dug into her purse to get her last twenty, and walked back to the deli.

"Hey Jon," she said as she slipped behind the counter. She went to work on making some fresh sandwiches, then poured three iced coffees. She loaded them up on a tray and carried them outside.

"Hello," she said, lifting her hand to knock on the side of the van door.

Colt pulled it open. "Howdy, ma'am."

"Oh," she said, surprised to see him standing there, like he'd been waiting for her.

He grinned. "I saw you coming."

"You're supposed to be watching the customers, not Emery," a hard voice said from behind.

Ignoring Luke, Colt looked at the sandwiches. "Am I ever glad to see you."

"That's because I brought you food."

"Darlin', you could be standing there empty-handed,

completely naked of...everything...and I'd still be happy to see you."

"You are trouble, aren't you?" she responded. "Maybe Luke was right. Maybe I should have stuck with him."

She looked past Colt's shoulders and a fine quiver moved through her when she found Luke's intense gaze fastened on her. He went as still as a stealth soldier, and the air around them seemed to charge, come alive with energy. With his focus one hundred percent on her, every nerve in her body tingled, crackled, moisture breaking out on her skin.

"I...I thought you guys could use something cold to drink and I noticed no one stopped for a lunch break, so I..." She stopped speaking and held the tray out.

"Beautiful and thoughtful." Colt licked his lips and took the tray from her, but he was looking directly at her when he added, "Delicious. Damned if you aren't my kind of girl."

Something flickered in the depths of Luke's eyes. "You didn't have to do that."

"I wanted to."

He studied her for several long seconds, longer than what was comfortable. Something passed in his eyes, but she wasn't sure what. He briefly closed them, and when he opened them again the ghosts were back. She turned to leave, and while she didn't know what that look meant, she could feel his gaze burning into her back, like he was in the battlefield tracking his enemy's every move through his crosshairs.

———

As they all kicked back at Sky Bar, enjoying a cold beer and meal after a long day, Colt let loose a long slow whistle. "Damn, she's hot. Real sweet too." He adjusted his Stetson and glared at Tanner. "More my type than yours though, old man."

"Like hell she is," Tanner shot back as he turned the brim of his Texas Rangers cap backward, like he was itching for a fight. Clearly the two had been spending too much time together in a hot van.

Luke leaned back in his chair and linked his fingers around his neck as Colt and Tanner battled it out over Emery and who was more suited for her. Not that Luke would let either of them get too close.

Shit.

What the hell was he worried about that for? She wasn't his, and she wasn't his type. In fact, they were complete opposites. He didn't belong in her world any more than she belonged in his. He looked around the bar at all the rough and rugged soldiers who had all been to battle, ready to give their lives for their country. Yeah, she'd be completely out of place here, and the men from her world likely wore expensive suits and designer shoes, not fatigues and combat boots.

He spotted Matt at the bar, reading over his MCAT books and stealing glances at Sky. Luke's gaze shifted to the blonde who'd been eyeing him last night. Damn, he should have just taken her home. Should have buried himself in her and forgotten all about Emery. Sweet Emery who brought them food and drinks, and then paid for it herself. Yeah, he saw her drop the money into the cash register. He'd be damned if he'd stand for that, or take anything from the Taylor family. That money would come off the end contract.

Garrett sat next to him, his beer bottle hitting the table hard and pulling Luke's thoughts back. His friend gestured toward Colt and Tanner. "Who are these two clowns talking about?"

"Emery," Luke said, then took a long pull of his own beer.

"Your Emery."

"She's not my anything."

"Yeah, I can tell."

"You should wipe that smirk off your face before I do it for you," Luke said.

Garrett laughed and slapped Luke on the shoulder. Then he pulled his hand back like grenade had just gone off. "Jesus, that hurt."

"What hurt?"

He shook his hand. "I hit that chip on your shoulder. It's a big muthafucker. I damn near bruised my hand."

Luke glowered into his bottle. Yeah, so he had a chip on his shoulder. Who could blame him? He hated rich people who thought they were better than everyone else.

"Do you know what she did?" he asked.

"What?"

"She brought us all food." He shook his head. "Did she think we couldn't afford it? Or maybe she did it because she figured I'd steal it if she didn't provide it."

"Or maybe she was just being nice, dumbass. Did you ever think of that?"

Luke planted his elbows on the table and fisted his hair as he thought more about her. Honest to God, she confused the hell out of him.

"I told you, she wasn't the one who had it out for you."

"Doesn't matter."

"No?"

"I don't want her and she doesn't want me. So this conversation is a waste of time."

Garrett looked at Colt and Tanner again. "That's probably a good thing, because it looks like you'd have to fight those two for her."

"They act like an old married couple," Luke said, but at least he trusted them and they were both damn good at their job.

"I guess working closely with her is really getting to them."

"Seems that way."

"And she's not getting to you?"

"Nope. I have a job to do and as soon as I'm done, I'm out of there."

Just then the cute blonde started sauntering his way. She looked as sexy as hell in a flannel shirt tied at the waist and tight, low-cut jeans that showcased her curvy hips. A broken-in pair of cowboy boots climbed up her long legs and completed the farmer's daughter look.

But it's not the farmer's daughter you want...

Shit.

Before the girl reached him, he leaned forward, and said, "Hey you two. Knock it off. Emery is the boss, and we don't chase the boss. Got it?"

"Since when?" Garrett asked, turning those sharp eyes on Luke.

"Since now," he answered, knowing Garrett was thinking about Luke's fling with Shari. Sweet and sexy Shari. She was the artsy type and owned Jewelry is Forever, a small boutique store where she sold specialty jewelry that she personally crafted. When she discovered a lot of it was going out the door unpaid, she'd hired his company to set up a security system. She was a sweet thing, if not a little on the flighty side, and after his first day working for her, he found himself in her bed. She was fun, free spirited, and their affair lasted as long as the job. Ironic really, because to her Jewelry was Forever, but relationships weren't. Not that he wanted anything more with her, anyway.

"Hey there," the pretty girl said.

Just then Colt and Tanner stopped arguing and snapped to attention like any good soldier.

"Hey," Luke said in return, relaxing back in his chair, despite the grin Garrett was casting his way.

Curling a long strand of hair around her finger, she

gestured toward the bar. "How would you like to buy a girl a drink?"

"I would," Colt said.

"Me too," Tanner piped in.

She cast a smile their way, then turned back to Luke. "How about you?"

"Sure," Luke said. He picked up his beer and climbed to his feet, ignoring Colt and Tanner's mumbled curses. "What are you having, sweetheart?" he asked as he guided her to the bar, and away from prying eyes.

"Daiquiri." She smiled. "And the name is Daisy."

Of course it was.

He sat across from her, ordered her drink, and after some twenty minutes of listening to her talk about the cute pair of shoes she found last week, he glanced at his watch.

She touched his chest, clearly reading him wrong. "Is it time to go?"

"Yeah," he said.

She offered him a dazzling smile, showing off perfect white teeth as she shimmied closer. Christ, what the fuck was wrong with him? Any other day he would have taken her home, but tonight, well, he just wasn't in the mood. Which was bat shit crazy, because he was *always* in the mood.

"I have somewhere to be," he said.

"Me too." She flashed her dark lashes, and pouted her lush lips, a look she probably perfected in the mirror.

"Sorry, sweetheart." He inched back and stole a glance at his watch. "But I have to finish up some work."

She eyed him suspiciously. "I thought your work day was over."

"Yeah, but this job's been a real bitch." She glared at him. "Listen." He pointed to Colt and Tanner. "Those two are good guys."

She looked past his shoulder, then ran her fingers down

his chest. She pouted for a minute then said, "Fine, but next time you're not getting off so easily."

Luke gestured for Colt and Tanner to come over, and they both leapt from their chairs like well-trained lapdogs. Luke smiled, wishing he could stick around and watch them duel it out over Daisy.

He introduced them, then told the guys he had some last-minute work to take care of. They both gave him an odd look but said nothing. No way in hell were they going to call him on it and jeopardize a chance at spending the night with sexy Daisy.

The night was still early as he made his way to the door, and just as his palm closed around the knob, Garrett's hand landed on his shoulder.

"Yeah, it's real clear she's not getting to you."

Shit.

Luke jumped onto his bike, pulled on his helmet and made his way through the city streets. Perhaps a good hard ride would clear his head. He had no idea where he was going but when he found himself on the other side of the street from Taylor's Market, he shook his head, knowing he was good and fucked.

The girl *was* getting to him.

The Closed sign was in the window and the lights were dim. He sat there for a moment longer, when he spotted movement inside. What the hell? He stole another glance at his watch. The store closed at eight and it was fifteen minutes past. He supposed Emery could still be inside and was about to go investigate when the door opened and Emery came out. Holding a big paper grocery bag in one arm, she punched a number into her phone. Talking and walking and looking completely distracted, she cut the corner and hurried down the street.

Luke started his bike and followed behind, wondering

what the hell she was doing. As she made her way farther south, turning down one of Austin's more dangerous streets, Luke's heart thumped. What the fuck was she doing out here at night? This was no place for her to be walking alone. From the shadows, Luke saw a movement, two men moving toward her. Every instinct he possessed came out full force and prompted him into action.

He started toward her on his bike, ready to put himself between her and the approaching men.

With her phone braced between her shoulder and ear, she shifted the grocery bag, completely oblivious to him behind her. She stepped off the sidewalk as the shadows moved closer. Halfway across the dark street, her phone slipped from her ear, and as she fumbled with it, a car came around the corner and headed straight for her.

She was so damn distracted that she hadn't even seen it coming. Luke revved his bike and sped toward her. He didn't get there fast enough, however. The car skidded to a halt, but not before bumping into her. She cried out and fell to the ground.

Jesus Christ.

Luke was off his bike in seconds flat. "Emery," he said. He ran to her and dropped to his knees. She blinked up at him and a measure of relief moved through him to find her conscious. He leaned closer, his eye assessing hers. "Emery, are you okay?"

The man jumped from his car. "Is she okay? I didn't see her. She came out of nowhere."

"Call an ambulance." Even though Luke wanted to punch the guy in the throat, he didn't want to take his eyes off Emery. She groaned and continued to blink up at him, a confused look dancing in her eyes.

"Luke?"

He clenched his jaw, worried that she had a concussion. "Yeah, it's me."

"What's going on?"

"You got hit by a car." She made a move to get up. "Don't move. You're confused right now. I think you have a concussion."

"I'm not confused. I didn't bang my head and I know a car hit me. The only thing that's puzzling me is you and what you're doing here."

Instead of answering, and telling her that he couldn't seem to get her off his mind, he clutched her arm. "Let me help you." He raised her a bit, and put his hand on her lower back to help her sit.

"I'm okay, really. It was just a bump."

The driver started picking up her groceries and putting them back into her bag. "I'm so sorry," he said. "I didn't see you there."

She sat up straighter, and looked embarrassed as she searched the ground. "I wasn't paying attention. I was on the phone with the center, and it slipped..." She frowned when she found her phone smashed. "It's broke."

"I'll replace it," the man said. He dropped down next to her and handed her the grocery bag. "I'm so sorry. There's an ambulance on the way."

Emery blinked up at him. "I don't need an ambulance. You just bumped me and I fell."

"Are you hurt?"

"Only my pride," she said, and glanced at her knees.

The man smiled. "I'm Ethan Lane."

"*The* Ethan Lane?" Emery asked, looking back at him with wide eyes.

He laughed. "Just Ethan." he pulled a card from his wallet and handed it to her. As she narrowed her eyes and read it in the dark, Luke took note of the man's clothes and expensive car.

Who the hell was *the* Ethan Lane anyway?

"Emery Vincent," she said. "And I really don't need an ambulance. I just want to go home."

"Can I drive you?"

What the hell? No fucking way was she getting into the car with some stranger.

"I've got her," Luke said.

They both looked at Luke, and Lane angled his head. "Aren't you on a motorcycle?"

"Yeah, and I never hit anyone with it, either." Lane opened his mouth but Luke cut him off. "She's coming with me."

"Emery?" Lane asked. "Do you know this man?"

She nodded, as Luke carefully helped her to her feet. He towered over the other man and put on his best soldier's face. "We've got your information. You'll be hearing from us."

"I look forward to that," he said turning to Emery. "I'm so sorry. If you need anything, anything at all, call me. Even if you don't need anything, you can still call."

You've gotta be fucking kidding me.

The guy hits her then hits *on* her.

"I'd better cancel the ambulance then, if you're sure you don't need it."

"I don't need it."

He pulled out his phone as Luke moved Emery to the sidewalk. After Lane hung up, Luke stood there glaring at him until he got back into his Lexus.

"I don't like that guy."

"That's Ethan Lane, as in Lane hotels. He's one of the richest men in Austin. I think he was also in *Forbes'* '30 under 30'."

"I don't care who he is. I don't like him."

"The accident wasn't entirely his fault, you know. I was on a dark street, dressed in black and paying more attention to my phone than where I was going."

"Doesn't change a thing."

He turned to her and looked her over. She was shivering slightly, despite the heat of the night, and her hair fell into her face. He brushed it back, his fingers grazing her jaw. "Maybe you should get checked out."

Her voice sounded breathless when she answered with, "I don't need a doctor."

He looked her over for another minute. "If you're not okay to ride on my bike, I'll call us a cab."

She looked at his bike. "Honestly, Luke, other than my scraped knees and a bruise here and there, I'm fine. I can even walk home."

"You're not walking home." He grabbed her grocery bag, and led her toward his bike. He set the bag on the ground, helped her on, and positioned her feet on the foot pegs. As she adjusted her skirt between her thighs, he bit back a groan and put his spare helmet on her head. Her warm breath rasped across his arm as he adjusted the straps. "Okay?" he asked, giving a little tug to make sure he didn't have it too tight.

She shook her head. "Seems okay."

"What's your address?"

She gave it to him, then he grabbed her bag, hopped on in front of her and placed it between his legs. He angled his head and waited for a moment as she sat there with her hands on her knees.

"You need to hang on, sunshine."

"Oh, okay," she said and glanced down like she was looking for a handle.

He grabbed one hand, wrapped it around his stomach, then did the same with the other. She leaned against him and he tried not to think about the warmth of her thighs on his body, or how her skirt was riding up as she linked her fingers together. *Jesus.*

He turned around and headed back toward her market. He passed it and took a few more streets until he stopped in front of her very upscale townhouse.

He killed the ignition and braced his feet on the ground. Before he could help her, she climbed off the bike. Damn stubborn woman.

She fumbled with the helmet strap, trying to get it off.

"Come here," he said. He grabbed her apron and tugged her close. "There's a clasp right here." He took her hand and placed it over the release, to show her how to do it. Keeping his hands on hers, she loosened the straps, then pulled the helmet off. He took it from her and when big blue eyes met his, he said, "You shouldn't be walking in that part of town alone."

She glanced at the bag between his legs. "I had some deliveries to make."

"Deliveries? No one on that end of town is calling for deliveries from your market, Emery." He eyed her curiously, waiting for another explanation. He didn't get one so he opened the bag to peek inside.

She snatched it from him. "Thank you for seeing me home." She rushed up the three steps leading to her townhouse and fished her key from her purse.

He climbed off his bike and met her on the steps. "I'm seeing you in."

With her key dangling from her hand she swallowed, and for a moment she looked like she was about to argue.

"Open the door."

She slipped the key in the lock, and pushed the door open.

He followed her in and flicked on the light beside him. "Where's your bathroom?"

She gave him an odd look then pointed. "Down the hall, second door on the left."

He took the grocery bag from her, and set it on the small side table near the door. Then he grabbed her hand, and took her to the bathroom with him. He pointed to the edge of the tub. "Sit."

"Luke—"

"Sit down." He opened her medicine cabinet and rooted around inside until he found what he wanted. "If you're not going to get checked by a doctor, then you're going to get checked by me."

"You?"

"Yeah, I've had training in the field."

She angled her chin. "Do you always go through other people's stuff?"

He opened a small cabinet and pulled out a washcloth. "Are you always this stubborn?"

She looked down, and something passed over her face. His throat tightened, her look reminding him that she'd been strong for too long.

"What's the center?"

Her head snapped up. "What?"

"You said you were on the phone with the center."

She nibbled her bottom lip, drawing his attention to it. Fuck, he wished she wouldn't do that.

"It's a place where my brother lives." He stayed quiet waiting for her to continue. "I was supposed to visit tonight, and called to let them know I was going to be late."

"You better call and tell them you can't make it."

She nodded, and he was about to ask more questions when she turned the conversation to him. "Do you have any siblings?"

"Yeah," was all he said. He cranked on the hot water, wet the cloth, then dropped down between her legs. "Can you lift your skirt?"

She touched the hem, her fingers lingering there for a moment as she stared at the washcloth. "I can do it myself," she said.

"So can I and I've had training, remember?"

She inched her skirt up a tiny bit, and that's when it occurred to Luke that he had to be some sort of damn masochist. What the hell was he thinking? Being this close to her, between her long gorgeous legs, no less, was an exercise in frustration. His cock jumped, warning him that he was setting himself up for failure.

He coughed to hide the moan rising in his throat.

"You okay?" she asked, her knees clenched tightly together.

"Yeah." He lightly brushed one knee, removing the small pieces of gravel. She winced. "Sorry."

When he went to work on the other, she leaned forward and her hair flared around his face. "How does it look?"

"You're scuffed a bit, but once I clean and bandage it, you should be okay." He ran the cloth over her again, and her knees relaxed. He slowly widened them, and he was almost certain he noticed a change in her breathing as he washed and checked for injuries in between her legs.

He set the cloth aside, and grabbed the alcohol. "This is probably going to sting a bit too." He poured the alcohol onto a cotton ball and dabbed it onto her raw flesh. She let go of the hem of her skirt, and gripped the edge of the tub. He cast her a quick glace. "Okay?" She nodded, and trying to lighten the mood, he said, "You're kind of tough."

"Maybe you're just good at what you do?"

Damned if he didn't want to show her what he was really good at.

When he looked back down her skirt had slipped over her knees. As she continued to squeeze the tub, he slid his hand under the hem, pushing it up, just a tiny bit higher than she had it before. His hands trailed along her creamy thighs, so soft and smooth that all he could think about was widening them even more and running his tongue over her, tasting her sweetness as his mouth traveled higher and higher, to the warm spot that had been pressing against his lower back on the ride over.

"Jesus," he cursed, and clenched down on his jaw to get his shit together.

"What?" she asked, sounding breathless.

Not realizing that he'd said that out loud, he looked up at her, and when he saw desire reflecting in her eyes, it became his undoing.

He looked at her mouth, and she wet her bottom lip with her tongue, like she was preparing her mouth for him.

Walk away, dude. Just walk away.

A long strand of hair fell forward, and her warm, sweet scent reached his nostrils, shattering his last vestige of control. He wanted to fuck her. Wanted to push her skirt up over her hips, tear off her panties and pound into her so hard and so fast that he forgot she was one of *them*, that they didn't belong together. His blood pulsed as sexual heat flooded him, driving every sane thought away.

Sexual tension arced between them and engulfed the room. Hanging like fog, it was thick and heavy enough to obscure a battlefield and camouflage the enemy. His glance moved over her face, and every reason for staying away from her suddenly seemed so insignificant.

Why was sleeping with her a bad idea?

His hands traveled higher on her legs and his desire for her mounted as she leaned into him. Just one taste. That's all he'd take. One simple taste.

Her mouth parted, and some small part of him registered that she wanted this too. She wanted him. It made no sense, really. Unless she liked the idea of sleeping with the bad boy from the wrong side of the tracks. Maybe in her eyes, he wasn't good enough for her, but good enough for sex.

Unable to think about that as his tension grew, he drew the tang of her arousal into his lungs as it saturated the small room. His breathing became rougher, harder as he pressed between her legs, grinding his hard cock against her softness and knowing only a slip of silk stood between his mouth and her pussy. Her face flushed. Damn she was so beautiful.

"Emery," he whispered.

The soft rasp of her voice filled him with lust, when she said, "Luke."

The second he heard his name on her lips, he knew he was done for. He slid his hands through her hair, cupping the back of her head. Her lashes fluttered as he drew her mouth to his.

Their lips joined and his senses exploded as she opened for him. *Honey.* She was as sweet as fucking honey. His cock pressed against his jeans, begging for release. He gripped her hips and shuffled forward on his knees, positioning himself deeper between her thighs. His cock throbbed against her heat, and their moans mingled. His mouth pressed hungrily, greedily, his tongue slashing against hers, eager to taste every inch of her. She kissed him back, and her hands slipped around his waist.

She touched him, tentatively at first, but as their kisses grew more passionate, more heated, she ran her hands over his shoulder blades and through his hair. He could feel her hard nipples, and he knew he needed to get her naked so he could help himself to a taste.

His muscles bunched, his cock ached and he needed to take full possession of her. "Your room. Now."

He was just about to pick her up and carry her to her bed where he could ravish her all fucking night long, when the bathroom door creaked open. The unexpected noise caught his attention and he instantly switched to soldier mode. *Who the hell...?* He pulled back, and looked over his shoulder, completely unprepared for what happened next.

He ducked as a big black ball of fur jumped over him, landing squarely on Emery's lap. *What the fuck?*

"Jinx," Emery said, running her hand over her cat. "What are you doing?"

Jesus.

With the mood broken, he looked at her and worked to steady his racing heart. "You have a cat," he said, stating the obvious.

She gave him an apologetic look. "She was just curious. I don't usually bring men..." She stopped talking and angled her head as he glared at her cat. She removed the black ball from her lap and shooed her away, like she was ready to pick up where they left off. Luke went back on his heels, and she frowned. "You don't like cats?"

"I'm a dog person." As he watched the feline rush into the hall, it once again reminded him they were very different people, who came from very different worlds, and that kiss never should have happened. "And I...uh...I should probably finish up with your knee and go check on my dog."

"Okay," she said. Her voice was light, but she couldn't disguise the hurt in her eyes. It hit him like a sucker punch and he felt like a world-class prick for backing away from something he never should have started in the first place.

4

Emery spent most of the day in her office, unable to face Luke after that amazing kiss the night before. Things had been going so well until Jinx came along and scared him off. But it was more than just her cat that had spooked him. She had caught that haunted look in his eyes again, and felt the quiet, controlled anger just below the surface.

The knock on her door pulled her from her thoughts and she glanced up to see Mr. Lane...Ethan standing there smiling at her. Shocked, she jumped to her feet.

"Ethan," she said, her glance moving over his handsome face, and dark suit. "What are you doing here?"

"I owe you a phone." He held a black box out to her. "And I thought maybe I could take you to lunch."

"Thank you so much." She took the box, touched that he'd done this for her. Honestly, no one had ever given *her* anything before. "But you didn't have to do this, and lunch isn't necessary."

"Of course I did, and yes it is." He glanced over his

shoulder then lowered his voice. "I also wanted to make sure everything went okay last night after I left you."

Her mind took that minute to rush back to the bathroom and way Luke had touched her. His rough hands on her knees, her thighs, climbing higher and higher, until he almost reached the spot that needed him the most. Everything in the hungry way he touched her left her breathless, desperate for more. She could feel heat rising in her face and hated how she wore her emotions on her sleeve.

She swallowed past the tightness in her throat, and worked to find her voice. "Yes. Everything went fine." She narrowed her eyes. "Wait, how did you know where to find me?"

He smiled, a smile so bright and dazzling it probably charmed everyone in the business world and played in his favor. "You were wearing an apron that said *Taylor's Market*."

"Ah, right. I forgot." She opened the box and pulled out her phone. Seeing that she had one contact she clicked on it and grinned. "I see you programmed your number in."

"Like I said, you can call me anytime. So about lunch?"

A movement behind Ethan caught her attention, and she looked over his shoulders to see Luke standing there. A rush of sexual energy hit her. Their gazes clashed and he clenched his teeth, the muscles along his jaw rippling.

"I didn't realize you had company," Luke said.

She held the phone out. "Ethan stopped by to replace my phone." A wave of guilt moved through her as she rushed to explain. Which was silly, really. It's not like he wanted her, and Ethan was being very kind, replacing her phone and coming to check on her.

Ethan turned to Luke and held his hand out. "I never did get your name last night."

"Luke Phillips," he said, a hardness in his tone as he gave the man a quick shake. He turned to Emery. "I need to get into your office to install some equipment. If you're going to lunch, then maybe now is a good time."

She looked at him for a moment and could feel the tension pouring off him. "Maybe I should stay." She looked at Ethan. "Luke might need me for something."

"Nope," Luke said quickly. "I don't need you for anything."

Her stomach clenched, his words hitting like a slap. What the hell was going on with him? One minute he was kissing her, ready to take her to her bed, and the next he was back to hating her.

"Okay." She turned back to Ethan, who was looking at Luke curiously. "I'll just grab my purse."

Ethan stepped to the side to let Luke pass with his box of equipment. Ignoring them, and whistling to himself, he started on his work.

"My car is out front," Ethan said, clearly feeling the tension every bit as much as she did. "I'll meet you there."

Emery walked to the safe behind her desk and started to open it.

"Are you sure you want to do that with me in the room?"

She turned and glared at him. "Is there a reason I shouldn't?"

Luke shrugged, but underneath that hardness she spotted something else, something that looked like a deep, unyielding pain. "You tell me," he said, turning his back to her as he strung wire.

Emery's heart pounded. "Luke," she began cautiously. "About last night."

He turned to her then, his eyes so dark and intense as they latched onto hers, she nearly fell back into her chair. "It shouldn't have happened. I shouldn't have..."

"I was there too," she said quietly. "You're weren't in it alone."

He looked at her like she was a game of chess and he was trying to figure out his next move. Then something in his face softened.

"Emery..."

Heat arced between them, and she took a step toward him.

"Don't do that," he said.

"Do what?"

"Don't come so close."

"Why?"

She stepped closer, despite his warning. "Because I'll want to kiss you again."

She swallowed. "Maybe I want you to." One more step closed the distance between them, and something dark and tortured moved over his eyes when she moistened her lips.

He caressed her with his eyes. "Emery," he groaned, his throaty voice doing the weirdest things to her insides. He gripped her arms and dipped his head.

"It's just a kiss," she said, and her words seemed to do something to him. He leaned into her and swiped his tongue over her bottom lip. He licked her slowly, like he was savoring the taste of her. His body heat curled around her and she soaked it in as he looked at the ceiling and groaned, a deep, tortured sound from the depths of his throat. A second later his mouth crashed down over hers. Hard.

Desire twisted inside her, ripples of sensual pleasure sweeping over her skin. He deepened the kiss and gripped the back of her head to hold her against him. She reveled in the sweet taste of him as their tongues joined. It became harder and harder to draw in air as they devoured each other. Desperate to feel him, she ran her hands over his back.

The second she touched him he inched back, the kiss coming to a screeching halt. His breath came in a ragged burst as he stepped away. A barrage of mixed emotions moved over his eyes before he hardened himself. "You'd better go."

"What?" Confused, she stared up at him.

He fisted his hair. "Your lunch date, remember."

"I'm not sure..."

"No, you should go." He scrubbed his chin, that haunted look back in his eyes. "I'm not the guy you should be with." He waved his hand back and forth between the two of them. "And whatever this is..."

"...is nice," she said.

"Yeah, it's nice," he said quietly. "But it can't go anywhere."

"I never expected it to." She knew the rules, knew what she'd be getting herself into with Luke.

Luke opened his mouth like he wanted to say something, but when one of her cashiers stuck her head in and said, "I'm going on my break," he walked back to the monitors.

"You'd better go. I'm sure a guy like Ethan Lane isn't used to being kept waiting."

Of course she never expected it to go anywhere. He wasn't from her world. He never expected it to go anywhere either, but hearing her say it—pointing out the obvious between them—pissed him off a hell of a lot more than it should have.

With her out of the office he concentrated on hard-wiring her monitoring system. Every now and then he caught a whiff of her scent, and his mind went back to the way she felt in his arms. She was so fucking warm, so soft and pliable under his mouth, he was ready to take her right there, until she reached out and touched him. He loved the way her hands felt on his body, the way she splayed her fingers like she wanted to explore and acquaint herself with every inch of his body. His cock twitched just thinking about it.

Okay, so the way he saw it, he had two choices. One, fuck someone else to get his mind off of her, or two, fuck her. Even though being with her went against everything he stood for, there was no denying they both wanted each other.

With that last thought in mind, Luke focused on the task at hand. Close to an hour later, Luke's cell rang, and when he saw that it was Theresa, his secretary, he slid his finger over the screen to answer. "Hey, Theresa. What's up?"

"Shari, from Jewelry is Forever, called. She said she was having some static problems with her monitors."

Shari...

It was almost like a sign. Not only would sleeping with Shari get him over his hang-up with Emery, it would get him out of the store before Lane brought her back. Yeah, the timing for her call was perfect, just perfect.

"Okay, call her back and tell her I'll be right over." He hung up, walked through the market and hurried to the van.

"Hey, guys," he called out, sticking his head in the door. "I have to stop in and check on Shari. Apparently she's having some wiring problems. I'll grab us some cold drinks and lunch on my way back."

"Yeah, sure, boss man," Colt said, a smirk on his face. In fact he'd been in a pretty good mood all day, which led Luke to believe he was the lucky one with Daisy last night.

Luke glared at him. "What?"

"You tell us Emery is hands off and..."

Just then Tanner nudged him and he went quiet.

"You've got something to say, Colt?" he asked, squaring off with his comrade. Honest to God, he loved the guy, and he knew Colt was just razzing him, but for some reason he hated Colt thinking about Emery, or even talking about her. It made him want to beat the crap out of him. Shit. He needed Shari, and he needed her now.

"The only thing he's got to say is thank you for hiring his sorry ass when no one else would. Isn't that right, Colt?"

"Damn straight," Colt said, adjusting his Stetson. "We've got everything under control here. And make mine a Coke, will ya?"

"Sure thing."

Luke left them to work and walked to his motorcycle parked behind the van. He pulled on his helmet and was just about to slip into traffic when Lane drove past him and pulled in up ahead.

Emery spoke to him for a moment, then she got out of the car. Damn douchebag didn't even open the door for her. With a little finger wave, she started toward the store. Luke revved his bike and she turned to him. Their eyes met for a brief second, then he peeled out of his parking spot.

Twenty minutes later he pulled up in front of Shari's small boutique. He secured his bike and made his way inside, the bell overhead jangling when he entered.

Her face lit when she saw him. Just like old times.

"Luke," she said loudly, catching the attention of two teens who were trying on rings. "Thanks for coming by so quickly." She waved him closer, the bangles on her wrists clanging.

"What's up?" he asked, and she bit her lip playfully, a familiar gesture that spoke volumes.

Her glance dropped to his crotch. "You tell me."

Now if that wasn't an invitation he didn't know what was. They'd get to that, but first he needed to check her equipment—of the security variety.

"Theresa said you had static on your monitor."

She pouted. "Yeah, it's acting strange."

He stepped around the long counter, and a fan blew across

his face. No expensive air conditioning in this place. He dropped to his knees and looked over the monitor he had placed below the counter.

"When did the problems start?"

"Yesterday," she said, kneeling down beside him. She moved close, her body brushing up against him as her sweet familiar scent wafted before his nose.

"Have you banged it or moved it?"

"No, but Jamie was working last night and it's possible that she could have."

He pulled the monitor out and checked the wires on the back. "There we go. Looks like you just had a loose connection." He twirled it, and as soon as he tightened it, her screen became picture perfect once again.

"Well look at that. I fiddled with the dials earlier, but nothing happened. I guess you just have the right touch."

"It's my job to know what I'm doing."

"And you're *very* good at what you do."

As soon as the words left her mouth, he thought back to Emery and how she pretty much said the same thing to him when he was bandaging her leg. Emery. Ah shit. He somehow suspected even if he did take Shari to her bed, it would do nothing to get Emery out of his head. He was damned if he did and damned if he didn't.

She blinked long dark lashes at him. "Have you had lunch yet? I was about to lock up for the next hour."

He stood. "I have to run, I'm in the middle of another job."

"Oh, so soon. I was hoping you could stay for a bit. We always did make the best of our lunch breaks."

"I can't, Shari. I'm really busy." He walked around the counter. "Everything should be okay now but if you have any more trouble, just call."

"Bye, Luke," she said, waving him off and turning her

attention to the guy who'd just come through the door. Luke grinned, sensing she'd instantly found someone else to keep her occupied for the next hour.

He made his way back to the market and parked his bike. He was about to walk down the street when he saw Emery leaving the van.

Yeah, he was pretty sure he was going to have to fuck her. Swiping moisture from his forehead he walked to the van, and he frowned when he saw Colt and Tanner with a stack of sandwiches.

Colt took a big slurp of his soda, then gestured toward the small counter. "Dig in," he said.

Luke grabbed a sticky note and wrote down everything she'd delivered so far. "We're paying for this stuff," he said. "We don't take handouts."

"Whatever you say, boss man," Colt said.

The rest of the day sped by, and as Luke worked he thought about Trent, hoping he was going to show up at the center tomorrow. He planned to go by, to check on him, and the others he'd sent in the past, and if he wasn't there, he and Luke were definitely going to have words. Although something in Luke's gut told him the boy would show up.

When quitting time came around, Emery was still inside working. Tanner jumped behind the wheel. "You coming to Sky Bar tonight?" he asked Luke as Colt jumped into the passenger seat.

"Yeah, I'll probably stop by."

Colt suddenly looked sullen. "What's the matter with you?" Luke asked.

"Nothing."

Luke slapped him on the shoulder. "Don't worry, kid. Daisy is all yours."

With that Colt's face lit up, and Luke opened the sliding door. "I'll catch up with you guys later." In need of a shower,

Luke climbed on his bike, taking one last glance into the market before he called it a week. He pulled into Friday night rush hour traffic and made his way to his apartment. It was in a shitty part of town, but not as bad as where he'd grown up. After his buddy Brad Crosby moved into the old Victorian house he'd restored, with his new wife, Madison, Luke had taken over the lease.

He stepped inside and enjoyed the air conditioning Brad had installed in the window and left for him. Rex jumped from the sofa and came barreling over, his tail wagging hard.

"Hey, boy." As he scrubbed a hand over his Shepherd's head he looked around at his belongings, or lack thereof. He could only imagine what Emery would think of the place.

Sweet Emery who wanted him, and brought him food and drink. For a moment he thought about the underlying reason she'd hired him. Clearly she believed in his firm's work, but did she believe in him on a personal level?

"Want to go for a run?"

Rex's tail went faster as Luke grabbed the leash. A minute later they made their way outside, and as the sun set, the air cooled slightly. He took Rex to their favorite park and let him off leash. They ran the outskirts of the park, Luke keeping a close eye on Rex. He didn't want to overwork him and tire him out, especially since they'd both be working at the compound tomorrow.

Once Rex started to slow, Luke leashed him and they headed back to the apartment. He fed Rex, gave him a big bowl of water and walked to his fridge to get a drink for himself. After downing it, he took note of Rex fast asleep on the sofa. He grinned. The old boy spent more hours sleeping than anything these days. He walked past him and jumped into the shower.

After a good long scrub, he pulled on his boxer briefs and plunked himself down on his sofa next to snoring Rex and watched some mind-numbing television until darkness fell over the city. Deciding he needed to get up and out before he crashed for the night, he climbed into a clean pair of jeans and tugged on a T-shirt. He left his apartment, took the stairs two at a time and jumped onto his bike.

He started into traffic, making his way to Sky Bar, but decided to take the long way around. He drove by the market, wondering if Emery was still working, but when he saw her once again walking down the street, a shopping bag tucked under her arm, he cursed.

He followed her, determined to find out exactly what she was up to this time. Once again shadows came out of the woodwork, and while he wanted to get to the bottom of matters, he couldn't stand back and do nothing when her safety was at risk.

He revved his bike and pulled up beside her.

She turned toward him, and her eyes went wide.

"Luke?" she said, sounding breathless.

"What are you doing?"

She clutched the brown paper bag tighter. "I could be asking you the same thing."

"Okay, then I'm following you. Your turn."

"Why are you following me?"

"Answer my question first."

"I'm..." She looked into her bag. "I'm doing a delivery."

He stared at her, reading her body language. "Try again."

She lifted her chin slightly. "It's true." She looked behind her. "At least, I *was* doing a delivery until you scared them off."

Luke searched the shadows. "Scared who off?"

"If you must know, I was delivering the day-old bread to a few people." She shrugged, like it was nothing. "It gets thrown out anyway."

His heart nearly stopped beating, because he knew it

wasn't *nothing*, and he knew exactly what was going on. "What people?"

"Just some men my father banned from the store a few years ago."

"Go on."

She stepped toward him and lowered her voice so that whoever lurked in the shadows couldn't hear her. "They're good people. They're just hungry."

He braced one hand on his knee, and said, "Put the bag down and get on."

She gave a hard shake of her head. "Last night they missed out because—"

"Emery," he said, cutting her off. He stole another glance around. "I'm guessing whoever I frightened away is still watching and will get the food when I leave, right?"

"Yes, I suppose so."

"So get on."

When she hesitated, he reached out to her, grabbed her by her blouse and tugged her closer. As soon as she was close enough, he reached for his spare helmet and put it on her head. Even though he'd taught her how to use the buckle, he did it for her anyway. Once he finished he gestured to the bag.

"Now put it down. You're coming with me."

She set the bag down on the sidewalk, and he crooked his finger when she looked like she was going to hang around a moment longer.

"I'm not leaving you here alone."

"I come here every night. I'm fine."

"Yeah, well last night you weren't so fine. You got hit by a car."

"I was distracted."

"And I'm not taking a chance that you'll get distracted again. Besides, I don't like you out here by yourself. If you want to give away day-old bread, can't you make the exchange at the store, before dark?"

"If my father ever..." She stopped speaking and folded her arms. "Why are you doing this? Why are you following me?"

"Because you clearly need someone to watch out for you."

Going on the defensive, she shot back, "I've been taking care of myself since I was a child. I've pretty much mastered it."

"Then maybe it's time you let someone else do it."

He slipped his hand under the helmet clasp and urged her closer, until their helmets bumped. "I'm not leaving here without you."

"Fine," she said. "You can take me back to the store."

"I'll take you home."

"I'm not going home."

He stiffened and wondered if she had another date with that asshole Lane. Today he'd made her go out with him, and now he suddenly found himself ready to walk barefoot over a bed of nails to stop her. Fuck. Talk about a mood swing. Maybe he should check to see if he was menstruating, or better yet, head on over Sky Bar and get one of the guys to kick him in the ovaries.

5

"Where are you going?" Luke asked.

She hesitated for a moment. She had the sneaking suspicion that he'd insist on taking her. He continued to stare at her, those dark, gray eyes of his searching her face, and making her feel as if he could see right through her. Honest to God, she had no idea what was going on between them. One minute they were in a hot embrace, with Emery basically telling him she was up for a no-strings affair—even though it was probably a very bad idea—and the next she knew he was pushing her out the door to go to lunch with Ethan. She wished he'd make up his mind whether he hated her, or wanted to take her to his bed. Because clearly slipping between the sheets with her was on his mind. She felt it in his kisses and in his body when he pushed up against her.

"I'm going to visit my brother, so if you'll just drop me back at the market, I can get on my way."

"Is your car there?"

She didn't own a car. It was an expense she didn't need at the moment. "No," she said. "I've made other arrangements."

"Such as."

God, did he never let up? "I'm going to call a cab."

"No you're not. I'm taking you. Get on."

Sensing he wasn't going to drop it, and wanting to get to her brother before visiting hours ended at ten, she said, "Fine, you can drop me off at the doors."

"Address?"

She told him the address and climbed on. He waited for a moment, then reached for her hands and pulled them around his waist. Unable to help herself, she spread her fingers, wanting to feel all his hardness beneath her palms.

With the warm wind in her face she clung to Luke as he drove to the center some twenty miles outside of town. When he pulled into a parking space instead of dropping her off at the doors like she'd asked, she climbed off and reached for the fastener on her helmet. Except his big hands were there first. He gave a little tug to urge her closer, and when the juncture of her legs pressed up against his knee, he released the clasp to pull it off.

His knee moved. It was slight, but she noticed it, noticed the way he was nudging her legs open and positioning his in between. Oh, God, she was practically sitting on his thigh, practically rubbing herself on his hard muscles.

But instead of moving, she found herself smoothing her hair, and her breathing became a little wobbly as he sat there staring at her.

"Thanks," she managed to get out.

"You're welcome," he said, and the next thing she knew he was climbing off.

"What are you doing?"

"I thought I'd hang out inside. I'd rather wait in there than out here if you don't mind."

"You don't have to wait for me. I can call a cab. It's what I always do."

He rolled one shoulder. "And I can wait for you."

Truthfully, while she secretly liked the idea of him waiting for her and taking her home afterward, she wasn't keen on him coming into the center. She had no idea how he'd react when he saw her brother. The men she'd dated in the past eventually learned about her brother's intellectual disability—or what the cruel school kids used to call retarded—and there wasn't one that ever wanted to talk about him, let alone visit the place with her.

"There's a lounge in the front lobby. You can wait there."

"Okay."

She began walking toward the doors, and he secured their helmets and jogged to catch up. Hyper aware of his hard body next to her and the sexual energy arcing between them it took all her concentration to put one foot in front of the other. She went to open the heavy glass door but he reached past her and gave it a tug. His hand moved to the small of her back and she caught his scent as he guided her in. God, the man smelled good!

She nodded to Sally at the front reception counter, then gestured to a chair. "I'll be a while," she said.

He picked up a *Good Housekeeping* magazine. "No worries. I've been meaning to catch up on this month's issue anyway."

Feeling his gaze on her back, she made her way down the hall and into the common room. All thoughts of Luke dispersed when she saw her brother, sitting in his favorite lounge chair and staring at the chessboard. Other center residents, as well as their visitors, were scattered throughout the room, playing board games or cards or simply watching the big TV on the wall with their loved ones. Two guards stood on opposite walls, keeping an eye on things.

"Jeremy," she said, lowering herself into the seat directly across from him.

His eyes lit when he saw her. "Em," he said. "Play."

"Of course."

She moved a pawn and looked her brother over. At first she hated the idea of putting him in here, but after her father's heart attack and Jeremy's increased aggression, she knew it was the best and safest place for him. He looked healthy and happy, and here he made many friends. No one stared or whispered names under their breath when he walked by. Even though externally he looked like a healthy twenty-seven-year-old, he really only had the mind of a child and sometimes his frustration came out in the form of violence.

Jeremy moved a piece and then began clapping. "I'll beat you," he said.

Emery laughed. "You always beat me."

They both made a few more moves, and Jeremy was surprisingly good at the game. After a while she let him beat her and he began clapping. A few of his friends came over, and they started rubbing his head and congratulating him.

With Jeremy distracted, she climbed from her seat, dropped a kiss onto his forehead and said, "I'll be right back. Next time I'm going to beat you, though."

"No way," he said. "I beat you."

Emery walked across the room and stepped up to one of the nurses. With her back to her brother, she spoke quietly to the nurse.

"How is he doing?" she asked.

"Emery, so nice to see you." Holding a clipboard to her chest, she looked past Emery's shoulders and smiled. "I see Jeremy beat you again."

"Always," Emery said, laughing. She lowered her voice even more. "Is the change in medication working?"

She touched Emery's arm. "The outbursts have calmed down, but he's been suffering headaches, which increases his anxiety."

Emery folded her arms, her heart heavy. She and her father used to take Jeremy on many outings, but with her father's failing health they could no longer remove him from the center and risk an outburst. The staff didn't like for her to take him out alone because there was no way to subdue him herself if he acted out.

"I'd really love to take him for a drive, just to give him a change of scenery."

"I know, but I don't think it's in your best interests. He's strong, Emery. As strong as any grown man, but he doesn't know his strength or how to control it."

Emery nodded. She wasn't hearing anything new, but it still didn't change the fact that her heart ached for her big brother.

"Oh," the nurse said. "Looks like he's found a new friend to beat at chess."

"What?" Emery spun around and her throat nearly closed when she spotted Luke sitting across from him. The big smile on Jeremy's face had her heart squeezing to the point of pain. "Luke," she whispered under her breath. "What the heck?"

"Is he with you?" the nurse asked.

With her throat so tight, all she could do was nod.

"Oh, my." She nudged Emery playfully. "You're one lucky girl."

She watched for a moment longer, watched the way Luke interacted with her brother, like he knew exactly what he needed. In that moment her thoughts raced back to Trent and how he handled him. Luke was really good with people. He knew just what to say, what to do to get them to respond to him. She was no exception.

As if feeling her eyes on him, Luke angled his head, and that old familiar half-cocked grin, the one she hadn't seen since he'd first offered to help her with her melons, curled up the corner of his mouth.

Heart pounding, she walked back toward them and tried to keep her voice light, casual when all the while her insides were nothing but a mixed bag of emotions.

"Watch him," she said to her brother as she pointed an accusing finger at Luke. "I think he cheats."

"Cheater, cheater," Jeremy said, mimicking Emery and pointing his finger at Luke.

He grinned, one eyebrow shooting up. "If I was cheating I'd be winning wouldn't I?"

Jeremy laughed and rubbed his head. "I always win."

Emery lowered herself into a chair and her heart swelled as she watched them. They continued to play, game after game and Jeremy continued to win. When the bell jangled, indicating that visiting hours were coming to an end, Luke pushed back in his chair.

"Okay, that's it. I give up. You're too good."

Emotions pressed against her chest when Jeremy jumped up and started clapping. There was nothing Emery could do to wipe the grin from her face as she climbed to her feet. She gave her brother a big hug and promised she'd be by again soon.

He waved her goodbye, and Luke stepped up beside her, his body close. They walked out together, silence hovering over them but she was so aware of his nearness, and the way her body was reacting. Sparks arced between them, and she was sure if someone lit a match they'd both go up in flames.

She was feeling breathless when they reached his bike. He grabbed his spare helmet and put it on her. The rasp of his fingers on her flesh turned her knees to liquid. He angled his head, his eyes on the clasp, and when his warm breath fell over her neck, her throat dried. She just stared at him, neither saying a word. He finished her buckle, and clicked his own as she climbed on. She watched his arms flex, the muscles along his back ripple. There was a new intensity about him, a dangerous kind of energy. It trickled along her flesh and raised the hair on her arms.

He started the bike, grabbed her hands to wrap them around him, and left the parking lot. She leaned into him, breathing in his scent as he drove her home. He pulled up in front of her townhouse and killed the ignition. She climbed off, her body a bundle of nervous energy, wondering if he would want to see her in again and what might happen if he did.

"Thanks," she said, her fingers fumbling slightly with the clasp. He watched her, his penetrating eyes sweeping over her features in a way that made her tremble.

Without speaking, he took off his helmet and climbed from the bike, leaving it parked on the sidewalk. He grabbed both helmets, then reached for her hand. Remaining silent, he held it tightly and guided her up the walkway.

When they reached her front door, she opened it. He stood there for a moment, his breathing a little heavier, his body a whole lot tenser.

"Did you...did you want to come in?" she asked, nervous and excited and needing him in her bed in the most inexplicable way.

He slipped a hand around her neck, and fisted her hair. "If I do, there will be no turning back this time," he finally said.

"What do you mean?"

"If I come in, I'm going to fuck you, Emery." His hand moved to her waist, pulling her up against him. His cock pressed against her stomach, letting her know in no uncertain terms what he wanted. "I'm going to tear your clothes off, put my hands and mouth all over your body, and then I'm going to take you. Hard." A wheezing sound escaped her lips. "So tell me, do you still want me to come in?"

As she found herself excited by the prospect, he stared down at her, his expression so dark, so hungry, she quaked from head to toe. Fearing her voice would fail her, she pushed her door open wider, broke the hold he had on her and stepped inside.

He tilted his head, his questioning eyes never leaving hers. Reaching out, she grabbed his T-shirt and pulled her in with him. A loud groan sounded as he followed her in. Standing in the entrance, he pushed her up against the wall, slamming and locking the door behind him.

His mouth crashed down on hers, hard, as he kissed her with a heat and passion. Grabbing her hands, he pinned them above her head and forced his knee between her legs to widen them. Longing ripped through her and she moaned—a deep, guttural sound that seemed to unleash something in him.

His mouth left hers and kissed along her neck. Warm hands ran down her sides, sweeping his palms along her breasts and stopping when he reached her hips. He pushed his knee harder against her pussy, shifting it back and forth, stimulating her clit in the most delicious ways.

"Oh, God," she murmured, her head falling to the side. Blood pounded through her veins and she wrapped her hands around his head, running her fingers through his hair as he kissed the hollow of her throat.

Fueled by need, she raked her nails over his back and wiggled her hips, shamelessly rubbing her sex against his thigh, wanting more...so much more.

"Fuck," he murmured.

Their bodies rocked against the wall and she tore at his shirt, wanting to touch and taste him all over too. A growl ripped from his lungs. He grabbed one of her legs and drew it around his waist, then slipped a hand around her ass to draw her up.

"Get on," he ordered.

She wrapped both legs around him and he pushed against

her, caging her between the wall and his chest. She couldn't decide which was harder.

Her entire body flushed hotly as every nerve sizzled. Sexual heat flooded her nether region as her body became pliable in his capable arms.

He tore his mouth from her neck and looked at her. His nostrils flared as perspiration broke out on his forehead.

"I need you naked. Now."

"My bedroom—"

"Too far." He carried her to the closest room, which happened to be her living room, and sat down on the coffee table with her still straddling him. She tightened her legs around him as he worked the buttons free on her blouse. He hissed air as he pushed it off her shoulders, letting it fall to the floor behind him. "You're perfect."

Her heart raced, loving the way he was looking at her, like she was the most beautiful woman he'd ever seen. Through the lace material of her bra, he ran his thumb over her nipples, and they hardened almost painfully. She arched into him, and with one hand he reached behind her back and expertly released the clasp. Her bra fell away and a tortured look moved into his eyes as her breasts spilled free.

His jaw muscles twitched. "So fucking beautiful," he growled, then swiped the soft blade of his tongue over one nipple, then the next. His wet heat felt like fire on her breasts, pulling a moan from deep within her.

Her thoughts whirled, unable to focus on anything but Luke and the way he was savoring her nipples. He sucked deep and twirled his tongue over her buds so hard and fast that she could feel the pull deep between her legs.

She raked her nails through his hair and held his mouth to her breasts as heat reverberated through her blood. Her thighs hugged him tighter and she shifted restlessly, needing him to touch her...*there*. Before she realized what was happening he was laying her out on the carpet in front of the hearth. His mouth slid downward, his tongue trailing a path over her quivering flesh. She listened to him breathe in her scent, and mumble curses under his breath.

He reached her pants and unhooked the button. A quiver moved through her at the hiss of her zipper as he lowered it. A second later, he jumped to his feet and made quick work of his own clothes.

Her heart raced as she took in his beautiful nakedness, all hard sinewy muscles that her fingers itched to touch, her mouth watered to taste. She looked at the sexy tattoo scrolls on his shoulders, then her gaze settled on his thick cock, so hard and ready. She loved how comfortable he was with his body and it secretly thrilled her to know how much he wanted hers.

Once naked, Luke sank to the floor and he moved between her legs. Dark eyes met hers as he began shimmying her pants down her hips and legs, leaving her in nothing but her panties. He tossed the pants away and pressed his mouth to her pussy, licking her through the slip of material.

"Luke," she cried out, and when she spread her legs in a silent invitation, his growl of pleasure thrilled her. "So good."

Taking her by surprise he grabbed the lacy band and tugged, ripping her panties from her hips. She gasped, but it quickly turned to a moan when he pressed a kiss over her pussy, dragging his tongue from bottom to top.

She caught the raw ache of lust in his voice when he said, "You're the sweetest thing I've ever tasted."

His thumb circled her clit, teasing, torturing, driving her deliciously mad. She shifted, trying to force him to touch her, and when she heard his soft chuckle she moaned, understanding he was purposely playing with her.

"Luke, please," she begged.

"Please, what?"

"Touch me."

His thumb skated over her clit. "Is this what you what? What you need so badly that you're willing to beg me for it?"

"Yes," she cried out and lifted her hips.

He placed his hand over her stomach to hold her down, then applied more pressure to her clit. It quivered and swelled, his deft touch sending shockwaves through her body. He gripped her legs and spread them wider and shot one last look at her before he lowered his head and buried his face in her pussy.

Never, ever in her life had a guy made it this good for her. She tossed her head from side to side, concentrating on the delicious pleasure between her legs.

He plunged two fingers inside her and pressed his palm hard against her clit. She nearly came off the floor, the pleasure so intense, so damn incredible she could barely catch her breath. Honestly, she never knew it could be this good. Luke was clearly as skilled in the bedroom as he was at his job.

She began trembling from head to toe, pressure building inside her as he took her higher and higher. Her body began tingling all over and her breath caught in her dry throat. She was close, so damn close, but he kept her hovering there, like he wasn't quite ready to bring her over.

"Feel with me," he said, taking her by surprise.

She lifted her head to find him looking at her, his gray eyes so dark and penetrating, her entire body trembled in response. He took her hand and gave a tug. She propped herself up on one elbow as he place her other hand on her clit, dragging her index finger back and forth, back and forth, ever so slowly. She'd never touched herself in front of a man before, but oddly enough she didn't feel embarrassed. In fact, it felt...erotic.

Their gazes remained locked and he said, "Feels good, huh?"

His sexy voice made her toes curl. She nodded and nearly sobbed with pleasure.

"No. Show me."

"Luke," she practically cried out as he plunged in and out of her, all the while rubbing her finger quickly over her clit. She grew tighter, slicker with each stroke, her body pulsing and throbbing as her climax approached.

"Oh, God," she cried out, her other hand gripping the carpet beneath her as everything inside her came to a peak.

"That's it, sunshine. Show me how good it feels."

Her muscles clenched hard around his fingers and he growled as she tumbled into orgasm. A second later he was between her legs, his tongue on her, in her, tasting her, drinking her in and prolonging the pleasure.

White-hot desire claimed her as he licked her and her muscles contracted harder, a whimper of sheer pleasure rising from her throat.

"So fucking sweet," he said before moving out from between her legs. He was about to climb up her body, but she reached between them and grabbed the hard length of his cock, desperate to touch him. She squeezed gently and dipped into the precome on his crown.

"Oh fuck that feels so good," he growled.

She ran her hands over his impressive length, reveling in his silky texture as he balanced on his arms. Her mouth watered. Never in her life had she wanted to taste a man as much as she wanted to taste him. Truth be told, she never really enjoyed giving oral sex before, but for some unknown reason, she couldn't wait to put him in her mouth, to lick every inch of his hardness.

She gave him a little nudge and he fell onto the carpet beside her.

"Emery," he whispered, as she settled between his legs,

her long hair spilling over his stomach. "Baby. What are you doing to me?"

She circled his crown with her tongue and he powered upward, his hands crushing her hair as she indulged in his body.

"Fuck."

She smiled inwardly, loving that she could make him feel this good. She angled her head to see him. Propped up on one elbow, he pushed her hair from her shoulders, like he wanted to watch her.

Turning her attention back to pleasuring him, and wanting to give him something to watch, she straddled one leg, rubbing her pussy on him as she took as much of him into her mouth as she could. When his crown hit the back of her throat, she cupped his balls for a slow massage and began sliding him in and out of her mouth. He grew impossibly bigger, stretching her lips as she devoured him.

She stayed between his legs, savoring, licking, tasting and never, ever wanting to stop, but she could feel his mounting desire and knew he was struggling to hang on. Soon his cock tightened and pulsed, and he gripped her shoulder to pull her off.

His eyes were clouded, his jaw rigid as he grabbed her. "I need to fuck you."

She sat watching as he grabbed his pants and pulled out a condom. Her body quaked with excitement, every nerve alive with anticipation as he tore into the package and slipped it on.

He lowered her to the floor and followed her down, bracing his hands on either side of her head as his mouth found hers. He settled his weight on top of her and she widened her legs even more, welcoming him to her body. The second she felt his crown breach her opening, she closed her eyes and ran her nails over his shoulders, anticipating the hard thrust.

"Look at me."

Her lids sprang open.

"You know what I'm going to do right?"

She nodded. "You're gong to fuck me. Hard."

"Yeah, sunshine," he said, the hunger in his dark gaze turning her inside out. "I'm going to fuck you hard."

His body fell over hers as he drove all the way into her. She gasped, but he swallowed it with a kiss. His mouth moved over hers, and he bit down on her bottom lip as he drove impossibly deeper. She circled her arms around him and began moving, pressing against him as he stretched her open.

"So good," she murmured between heated kisses.

He pulled almost all of the way out then impaled her again, slamming into her with such a force she thought they were going to go through the floor. But it didn't matter, because she loved every second of the way he was taking her, loved his intensity, his need, and the way he gave his all to everything he did.

His breathing changed, and moisture broke out on his flesh. Like a man hell-bent on grasping something just out of his reach, he pounded harder. In no time at all soft quakes began at her core, and she knew she was about to climax again.

"Oh, God," she cried out, her muscles tightening as she scraped her nails over his flesh, sure to leave a mark on him.

She let go, and opened her mouth, but this time no sound came. Heat whipped through her as her juices dripped down her leg.

He growled, pulled out and drove back in to her. "You're so fucking hot." She squeezed him, and he drew a shaky breath. "You've got me there, baby."

"Right where I want you," she murmured.

A growl ripped from his lungs as he threw his head back and let go. She could feel his cock pulse, his heart pound against her body as he climaxed deep inside her.

As she watched his jaw clench she knew he'd taken her beyond anything she'd ever known. Never in her life had sex been this good.

With his cock still buried inside, he collapsed on top of her, pressing her into the carpet. They stayed like that for a long time, just holding one another. Finally he inched back, and his expression was tender and hot when his glance met hers. As she basked in the afterglow, he brushed his knuckles over her face, everything in his touch warm, shockingly intimate.

"You okay?"

She nodded, going limp beneath him. "So...uh...yeah," she said. "That was ah..."

"Something I wanted to do since I first saw you juggling your melons."

She laughed, and said, "Yeah, me too."

His expression changed, worry moving into his eyes. "I didn't hurt you, did I? I knew it was going to be rough, because I needed you so fucking bad."

"It didn't hurt."

"Good. Next time, I'll go slower, I promise."

There was going to be a next time?

He rolled off her, discarded his condom, then moved in close. He propped himself up on his elbow and ran his hands over her stomach. She caught the mischief in his eyes, as his fingers began a slow climb.

"In fact, I think the next time is going to be sooner rather than later."

6

Luke blinked his eyes open and for a moment he had no idea where he was. A movement beside him had him turning. When he caught Emery looking at him, a small smile on her face, every hot memory from last night came rushing back in a whoosh.

He moved closer and dropped a kiss onto her mouth. "Morning, sunshine."

"Morning," she said, giving a lazy stretch. "What time is it?" she asked.

He moved his glance over her face. She looked so warm, so soft and welcoming. "Time for you to roll over and open up for me." He must have taken her at least a half a dozen times last night, yet he still couldn't get enough of her. All he could think about was being inside her again, pushing hard and deep and fucking her for the rest of the weekend. Good thing she had a box of condoms in her nightstand, considering how fast he burned through the couple he had on him.

A warm flush crawled up her neck as she rolled to her back and spread her legs wide. "See, not stubborn at all," she teased.

He pushed her sheets off and trailed his hand over her naked body. A shiver moved through her, desire backlighting her eyes. "I do love it when I get my way."

She placed the back of her hand over her forehead, and feigned distress. "The sacrifices I make."

Luke pushed a finger between her legs and swiped the rough pad over her clit, loving this playful side of her. She'd been under a tremendous amount of stress for too long, and it made him feel good to know he could help lighten her load and make her smile.

"Oh God," she cried out as she swelled beneath his touch.

He grinned and plunged inside to find her hot and ready for him. "Yeah, that's some sacrifice you're making, sunshine."

He leaned in and drew one nipple into his mouth, and her hands curled in his hair. She moved her hips, lifting them as he took her with his finger. His cock throbbed as he pushed another finger inside and pressed down on her clit with his palm. He worked her higher and higher and in no time at all she cried out his name and climaxed all over him. He loved how responsive she was.

He reached past her and grabbed a condom and, after quickly sheathing himself, he settled over her body. He braced his hands on either side of her head and hesitated for a moment. "You're not too sore are you?" He gave her a sheepish look. "I mean it's not like I was being rough or anything."

"I'm a little sore." He was about to back off until she cupped his face. "But I want you again." She drew his mouth to hers, wrapped her legs around his ass, and pulled him inside her. "As far as being rough," she whispered into his mouth, "I want you to take me the way you need me."

The second her heat wrapped around him he damn near lost it. Last night he'd promised her numerous times that he'd go slow, but what a load of crap that had been. There was just something about her that made him lose his shit, made him forget every sane thought but getting balls deep and fucking her hard.

He thrust into her, sinking into her warm, wet heat as he swallowed her gasp. She wrapped her arms around him and held him tight as he drove in and out, seeking, searching...needing.

She made a sexy noise and shifted, providing him with deeper access. He rammed into her, blocking everything from his mind except how fucking good it felt to be inside her. She was so soaked between the legs he easily slipped in and out, but the friction he was creating took him to the edge in record time. Raw desire seared his insides and he knew he was so damn close to falling over. Sensations whipped through him, and he bit back a curse, trying to hold on a little longer.

Her fingers dug into his back and she tossed her head to the side. He watched her face, loving the look that came over her as she peaked.

"So good," she murmured, the heat of her breath assailing his neck.

Her body began trembling beneath him, and her muscles clenched around his cock. A second later he could feel her wet heat sear his cock and pull his climax from him. He growled, and stilled inside her as she pulsed around him. Why was it so goddamn good with her?

"Fuck, yes," he bit out, then released inside her, giving himself over to the intense pleasure rocketing through him. She shuddered beneath him and he sucked in a quick breath as he settled his weight on top of her. When she began running her nails over his back, his entire body trembled. He loved the way she touched him like that.

He stayed there until his cock grew flaccid and the tension drained from his mind. Then he rolled off and discarded the condom before shifting back to face her. Her eyes looked sated, her grin satisfied when he shuffled back in beside her.

"Come here," he said.

Kicking the blanket to the end of the bed, he put his arm around her and she cuddled into him. Her hair flared around his shoulder and he tucked it beneath him. Lightly trailing his hand up and down her arm, he could feel sleep pull at him, but when she gave a low contented sigh it snapped him out of it. He looked down at her. While this was just about sex there was a part of him that wanted to know more about her.

"Tell me about Jeremy," he said. He felt her go stiff in his arms. He touched her chin, lifting it until their eyes met. His gaze moved over her upturned face. "What?"

"What do you want to know?"

"I don't know. Whatever you want to tell me, I guess."

Her gaze left his and she stared at the crack in her curtains, where morning light slanted in through the room. "He's a wonderful guy. So fun loving and so sweet, but a few years back, he became increasingly aggressive. Dad suffered a heart attack so Jeremy came to live with me. There was an incident, and I got hurt." Luke pulled her tighter, the need to protect her overwhelming him. "He didn't mean it, though. Sometimes he gets so frustrated and he doesn't know his own strength. I hated putting him in the center, but it's better for him. I see that now."

"It must be expensive."

Once again her shoulders sagged, like she had the weight of the world on them. "It is, which is why I need to get my market back in the black."

He brushed her hair back, understanding just how much she needed his help. "We will. I'll see to it."

She smiled up at him but he suddenly found himself unable to return it. Talking about her brother had him thinking of Allison. His heart clenched. The haunted look on her face after he was so cruel to her—telling her he *was* a thief and that he no longer wanted her in his life—still troubled him after all these years. A tremble moved through him.

"Are you okay?" she asked.

Not wanting to talk about his past, or his family, he said, "You seem like a really good sister. Jeremy is lucky to have you."

"I'd like to take him out to the park, or somewhere just to get him a change of scenery, but without my father's help I'm not able to take him alone. If he should have an outburst..."

"So you take care of your father, your brother and the market all by yourself." He went quiet for a moment, thoughtful, and wondered what she did just for her. "You have a lot of people counting on you."

"I don't want to let them down."

"Is that why you lied to your father about the security system?"

"I don't want him to worry."

He ran his fingers over her arm. "You know, you've been carrying the weight of the world on your shoulders for a long time. Maybe it's time for someone to take care of you for a change."

She gave him a sexy wink. "You just did."

As she teased him, trying to make light of the mood, he looked down at her, wanting to be the one to lighten her load and take care of her, at least for a little while. Soon enough the job would be done and they'd go their separate ways. But until then...

Turning the subject back to him, she asked, "You said you had a sibling?"

"Yeah."

"Are you close?"

"Uh, well, not really," he said. As soon as the words left his mouth, his stomach started to grumble, providing him with the perfect distraction.

Emery laughed. "I think we'd better eat. Maybe you picked up on some new breakfast ideas last night from that *Good Housekeeping* magazine you were reading."

He glanced at the clock. "While I'd love to stay and show you my culinary skills, which are magnificent I might add, it's getting late and Rex is probably bursting at the door."

"Rex?"

He pointed to himself. "Dog person. Remember?"

"Right."

He looked around. "Which reminds me. Where is Jinx?"

"Probably hiding somewhere." She gave him an embarrassed grin. "I think all the noise might have scared her."

"You mean she doesn't normally hear screams and cries coming from your bedroom...or living room...or bathroom?"

She whacked him. "Are you making fun of me?"

"Hell no. I did enough shouting of my own."

"That's true," she said, grinning. "You were a bit loud."

He laughed. "Just trying to keep up with you."

She drove her boney knuckles into his arm and he yelped as he glanced at the clock. "I'd better get moving. I have to grab Rex. We're heading out to the base together where my comrades train service dogs. Then I want to check on Trent at Sheffield Community Center."

She gave a heavy sigh, and her shoulders sagged. "I should probably get to the market anyway." She made a move to roll away from him, but on impulse he stopped her, pulling her back against him.

"Maybe you'd like to come to the compound with us," he blurted out without thinking. "I mean I know you're a cat person, but..."

An equal mixture of confusion and joy lit her pretty face. "Really?"

"Sure. If you can get away from the market for a few hours."

"I'd love to come. It's been all over the papers what you guys are doing and I'd be honored to see it firsthand."

"You would?" Shit. He was looking forward to spending a few extra hours with her, but he shouldn't be as happy as he was right now, considering this was a sex-only affair.

"Yeah."

He got quiet for a moment, thinking about everything she just told him about her family situation. "I have an even better idea."

"What's that?"

"Why don't we go get Jeremy? I bet he'd love the dogs, and then we can take him to Sheffield Community Center. The old folks there play chess and cribbage all day long. He'd fit right in." He winked and added, "And don't worry, I'll make sure he wins." Something passed over Emery's eyes, some deeper emotion that had his heart squeezing and thinking maybe he was crossing a line in the sand he knew better than to cross. Garrett's words suddenly came back to haunt him.

I messed in the wrong sandbox once. And look how that turned out.

She opened her mouth like she was about to say something, then closed it again. She looked at him, but with the way her eyes were glossing over, he guessed she was a million miles away.

"Unless..." he began. "Maybe it's a bad idea."

"Actually I really think Jeremy would love that." She gave him a big smile. "That's so sweet of you." He scrubbed a hand over his chin, wondering what the hell he was doing. She poked him in the chest, her smile falling. "Wait, unless *you* think it's a bad idea."

Of course it was a bad idea, but he couldn't tell her that now, nor could he back out after seeing how happy she was.

"I was the one that brought it up wasn't I? Let's get a move on it, before Rex leaves me a mess."

After showering, Emery dressed in a pair of jeans and light blue blouse that showed a hint of cleavage, while he crawled into the clothes he wore yesterday. Half an hour later they made their way outside and he took note of the way a few of her neighbors were staring at him with curious eyes as he climbed on his bike.

He gestured with a nod to the elderly gentlemen watering his flowers, two doors down. "I don't think he likes me."

"Good morning, Mr. Johnson," Emery said with a little wave. "And don't worry, he doesn't like anyone."

Mr. Johnson waved back, but Luke didn't miss the mistrust in his eyes. No doubt the man thought Emery was slumming with some motorcycle-driving thug from the wrong part of town, which of course, he sort of was.

As he drove he began questioning his sanity. What the hell was he doing? Seriously. They were different people from different worlds, and he shouldn't be taking her back to his place. One look at his apartment and she too would likely remember he was a world away from *the* Ethan Lane and run the other way. But what the hell could he do about it now? He'd put the offer on the table and she accepted it. The one thing Luke never did was go back on his word.

They pulled into his parking spot and she climbed off. She crinkled her nose at his bike. "How are we going to take Rex on a motorcycle?"

He pointed to his old pickup parked at the other end of the lot. "That's for Rex."

"You bought a truck just for your dog?"

"Yeah, but also to help transport the other shelter dogs as well."

She gave him a warm smile, and it was strange, because it made him feel all ridiculously happy.

"Come on, Rex is going to kill me for being late."

They hurried up the stairs, and when he opened the door, Rex started wagging his tail.

"Hey boy," Luke said, but he barreled past him to check out Emery.

She laughed and dropped to her knees as Rex began sniffing her all over. "I take it you smell Jinx on me," she said, rubbing his ears the way he liked. "I'm sure you two would get along just fine."

"A girl cat and boy dog. Oh yeah, they'll be besties," Luke said, tossing her a sardonic grin. "I'll be right back." He peeled his shirt off as he made his way to the bedroom and grabbed a fresh one from his drawer, then he climbed into a pair of clean jeans and met her back at the door.

She continued to pet Rex, but was glancing around his place with curious eyes.

"It's not much but it's home," he said, wondering why he felt the need to justify the place in her eyes. Truthfully, even if he did want more with her—which he didn't—he could never be the guy she'd want him to be, anyway—a guy like Ethan. All his money went to his sister's scholarship fund and to helping support the community center. But all in all, he was happy and didn't need much to live on.

Still down on her knees—which brought back way too many lust-filled memories from last night—she widened her arms and closed her eyes. "And you have air conditioning, which makes it perfect in my eyes. I think I need to get air conditioning at my place."

He watched her for a moment, a bit surprised by her reaction. His place was a shithole, of that there was no doubt, and he fully expected her to call him on it.

Maybe you brought her here to test her, some inner voice warned.

And maybe that inner voice could just go fuck right off.

"Come on. Rex is bursting." He grabbed the leash and stepped into the hall. But Rex was too busy smelling Emery to remember he had a full bladder. Luke tapped his leg. "Come on, boy." He still didn't move. "Emery, you'd better get out here, otherwise he'll stay there and sniff you all day."

She climbed to her feet and Rex followed her into the hall. They took him to the park and after he ran and played and emptied his bladder, they walked back to Luke's truck. Every now and then he cast Emery a glance, and he noticed she seemed a little lighter, a little happier. When was the last time she had a day away from work?

"Will you have to go in to the market today?" he asked.

She nodded. "I work every day."

They reached the truck and Luke opened the door. Rex jumped in and made himself at home. "You need to hire more staff."

She nodded. "I'm hoping once things start picking up I'll be able to bring in some part-time help."

Luke circled the truck and climbed in. He rolled down the windows, as Rex panted. "You hungry boy? You want breakfast?" Rex barked and Emery laughed.

"It's like he knows what you're saying."

"He does." He gave her a lopsided grin. "Every Saturday before we go to the compound he always gets a breakfast sandwich from McDonald's."

Her eyes widened. "You're kidding?"

"Nope, it's his treat."

Emery shook her head, and her scent reached him as her hair flared. Here he was berating Rex for wanting to sniff her all day, when he wanted to do the same.

"They can't be good for him," she said.

"You're probably right, but you know what, not only did he do two tours overseas, he's like a hundred years old. If he wants a breakfast sandwich he gets one."

She nodded and smiled at him. "I can see your point."

He pulled into traffic and a few minutes later he drove into the parking lot of Rex's favorite restaurant. "You don't mind eating in the truck do you?"

"Not at all."

"I don't want to leave him out here alone. I hate those bastards who lock their animals in their cars in the heat of summer. I once busted a window."

"You did."

"Damn right."

She grinned at him.

"What?"

"Such a rebel."

"Is that what you like about me?" he asked.

"Who said I liked anything about you?"

He reached over and cupped her sex. "You didn't tell me, sunshine, you showed me."

Grinning, and getting the full gist of what he was saying, she teased back. "Well, there are a couple of *little* things I might like."

"Little?" he asked.

"That's some ego you've got there," she said. Then she laughed and patted Rex. "I like that you're a good daddy."

Hearing the word daddy had him thinking of hers, which reminded him of his own and how he'd turned his back on him all those years ago. A wave of anger moved through him, but when Emery touched his arm, he exhaled slowly and looked past Rex's head to see her.

Her hand moved back to Rex, and she rubbed him gently. "Was it something I said?"

"Yeah," was all he said.

"I'm sorry."

"Nothing to be sorry for." He pulled his truck through the drive-through. "What will you have?"

"A muffin sounds good."

Luke put his order in and Rex whined when he got the whiff of food. "Don't worry. boy, it's coming, and then you get to play with Nana."

"Nana?" Emery asked.

"The only dog in the world older than Rex," he said, laughing. "She's such a sweet thing. I think Rex here has a crush on her."

"Was she a service dog too?"

"No, she was at Gemma's shelter, and when Gemma and my buddy Cole hooked up, they adopted her."

"I remember reading about Gemma's no-kill shelter in the papers. She's doing great things."

The food came, and Rex nearly leapt through the window to get his share. Luke held his arm out to hold him off. "Sit boy."

Rex reluctantly sat, and Luke pulled into a parking spot. He handed Emery a coffee. "Careful he doesn't knock it with his tail."

Emery fixed her coffee then bit into her muffin as Luke fed Rex, who ate his entire breakfast sandwich in three seconds flat, then turned to Emery to see what she had for him.

"Rex," Luke said, and he let loose a little whine and flattened himself between them.

He kept peeking up at Emery as she ate, and finally she said, "I can't take it anymore." She ripped a piece of her muffin off and Rex jumped up to gobble it down. "He kind of reminds me of you."

"Oh yeah, how so?"

"He somehow always gets his way."

As his mind rewound to all their lovemaking his cock shifted. He swallowed down the last bite of his sandwich and said, "Watch it there, sunshine, or we'll never make it to the compound."

They finished their breakfast and Luke gathered up the wrappers and tossed them into the garbage. "All set?" he asked, as she took a sip of her coffee.

She nodded and Rex settled himself in as he pulled onto the street. He turned a corner, making his way to the center, but decided to take the long way, something inside him compelling him to drive by his sister's place. He knew her schedule and really didn't expect to see her, but when he caught her rushing down the stairs of her apartment, he slowed to a near crawl.

He stayed back a few feet and just watched her. Dressed in a pair of cutoff shorts and T-shirt, she had her long dark hair pulled back into a ponytail. To him she was simply gorgeous. His heart pounded as she hurried down the sidewalk, a backpack over her shoulders. At the lights she met up with another girl, who had an armload of books, and Luke guessed they were headed off to study. They both chatted animatedly for a bit, then crossed the street and made their way to the coffee shop.

He swallowed, and the sound filled the cab. He shot a sidelong glance at Emery and noticed the way she was watching him. Her gaze went from his sister to Luke back to his sister again. For a minute he wondered if she'd question him. He also wondered if she'd recognize Allison from the photo he kept in his van. Yeah, he saw the way she had studied it with curious eyes. Then again, it had been taken a few years ago and Allison had grown up a lot since then.

Seconds before his sister entered the coffee shop, she looked over her shoulder and scanned the street, almost as if she felt his eyes on her. There was a haunted look in her eyes as they swept past his truck. He stayed still, perfectly still, then she turned around and stepped into the shop. He waited a second longer, then exhaled slowly before he continued on to the center.

Wanting to engage Emery in conversation before she asked a question he didn't want to answer, he said, "Do you think you'll have any trouble taking Jeremy out for the day?"

"Not once they see you."

"Yeah?"

"They just worry about my safety, and you're a big guy. If anything happens you'll be able to control Jeremy." She took a sip of her coffee.

He puffed his chest out. "You think I'm a big guy?" He cast her a sly glance. "Where do you think I'm big?"

"Jesus, Luke," she said, nearly spitting her coffee out. "Don't make me laugh when I'm taking a drink. And the biggest thing on you is your ego."

He laughed at that as Emery put her coffee in the cup holder. "I do wonder where we're going to put Jeremy, though."

"Don't worry, Rex loves riding in the back." He patted the seat. "And you can snuggle in next to me." As soon as the words left his mouth, he realized how much he liked having her sit beside him on the ride, how natural and easy she was to be with.

How much he wanted to fuck her again.

Fifteen minutes later, he pulled into a parking spot at the center. He leashed Rex in the back and they made their way inside. He stayed back and let Emery talk to the nurse, and when she cast him a big smile his heart thumped to see her so happy.

It had to be hard taking care of everyone else all the time, and once again he wondered if she did anything for fun.

He waited in the lobby and eventually she came out with Jeremy, who was grinning from ear to ear. Jeremy pointed at Luke and clapped.

"Cheater, cheater."

Luke laughed and put his hand on Jeremy's shoulder. While he wasn't as tall as Luke, the man was still solid. He could understand why the staff didn't want Emery to take him out alone.

"How about we go for a ride, and then later, I'll introduce you to some of my friends, who love to play chess. They're good but I bet you can beat them."

"I always win," he said and Emery took his hand in hers and walked with him outside. Luke stood back and watched for a second. There was just something about Jeremy that he liked and he had a feeling a few of the kids and elderly members at Sheffield would take him under their wings.

When they reached the truck, Rex stood and started wagging his tail. "This is Rex," Luke said. Jeremy leaned in and Rex gave him a big lick across the mouth.

Jeremy laughed. "Rex likes me."

"He does," Luke said, then turned to find Emery smiling at him. The way she lit up like a Christmas tree when he interacted with Jeremy did the strangest things to him. He turned back to her brother and let him get acquainted with Rex for a bit, then said, "Ready to go for a drive?"

After they all climbed into the truck, they made their way to the compound. Luke took note of the vehicles and was happy to see that Garrett wasn't there yet. Good. The last thing he wanted to hear was any more of his bullshit analogies. He and Emery were simply having sex. He might be playing in her sandbox but he wasn't looking to build anything. Even she so much as told him she didn't expect more. *Yeah, that's right*, he reminded himself. In her eyes he was a thief, one good enough to sleep with, but not to get involved with.

Luke opened the gate, pulled his truck through, and after they all climbed out of his vehicle, he shut it behind them. Emery took Jeremy's hand as he looked around nervously.

Luke gave her a questioning glance, but from the look on her face, he could tell she was worried about her brother's sudden bout of anxiety. Luke unhooked Rex and called Nana over. She sauntered slowly, and panted loudly as she made her way over to see Rex.

"This is Nana," he said to Jeremy. "She loves to be patted." Luke dropped to one knee. "Like this." He patted the ground next to him. "Can you help me, Jeremy?"

Jeremy looked at the dogs all running around and the equipment set up for training. He dropped down beside Luke and looked off in the distance to see Cole and how he was playing catch with Ralph.

Jeremy ran his hand over Nana's back and they all laughed when she rolled over and put her legs in the air. "She likes her belly rubbed," Jeremy said.

He rubbed her belly for a long time as Rex nosed around him, like he was in need of a bit of attention too. After awhile Jeremy pointed to Cole. "I want to play ball."

"Come on then. I'm sure Cole would love for you to help him."

Luke helped him up and as they made their way across the compound, Emery moved in close. Unease moved across her face. "You don't think the guys mind, do you?"

"No, sunshine. Trust me, these are the best bunch of guys you could ever know."

She relaxed into him, and without thinking he took her hand in his and gave it a little squeeze.

"Cole," Luke said when they reached him. "This is Jeremy, Emery's brother. He wants to help you with Ralph."

"Hey Jeremy," Cole said, and handed him the ball. "Just in time, my arm is getting tired."

Jeremy clapped as Cole's gaze zeroed in on Emery. Cole

did the introductions, and after his comrade turned his attention back to Jeremy, Luke nodded behind him. "Want a tour?"

"I shouldn't leave him."

"He's in good hands and right now, so enthralled with Ralph that he doesn't even know you're here."

She looked at her brother, who was smiling from ear to ear. "This is good for him."

Cole shot her a knowing glance. "I'll take good care of him," he said. "Don't worry."

With that she went off with Luke and he showed her all the work the guys were doing. He introduced her to every dog, and he suspected Jinx was going to have a fit when she got home.

After a complete rundown and a demonstration with Chester, they collected Jeremy and Rex and climbed back into the truck. Jeremy put up a bit of a fight, not wanting to leave, but Luke reminded him of the chess games he was going to play.

That seemed to appease him and put Emery at ease. They left the compound and headed to Sheffield. The heat of the day was upon them when he parked and he thought maybe Jeremy would like to go inside where there was air conditioning.

Emery climbed from the cab and as Luke freed Rex she glanced around. "So this is how you spend your Saturdays?"

"Mostly." A group of kids came running over when they saw Rex.

"Hey Rexy-boy," one of the girls said, giving him lots of love. She looked up at Luke. "Hey Luke."

"Samantha," he said as he handed her the leash. "Can you make sure he gets a drink?"

"You bet." The kids took off with Rex, his tail wagging like mad.

"They love him."

"He's a great therapy dog."

Emery grabbed Jeremy's hand and Luke grabbed Emery's. "Come on, let's get Jeremy settled then I'll show you around."

He guided them both inside, and Emery's eyes widened when he took her to a room where many elderly were lounging with young boys and girls, playing cards or chess. Everyone waved to him as he came in.

"You're popular."

"Especially with the ladies," he teased when Esther called out to him.

"Ego," she teased, whacking him lightly.

Jeremy looked around bright eyed and started clapping when he saw the chessboards. Luke settled him in with Frank, and once he was lost in the game, he grabbed Emery's hand to guide her out.

"I need to check and make sure Trent is here."

They walked back outdoors and he waved to one of the counselors who had a bunch of kids working on the vegetable garden.

"What exactly is this place?" she asked, her glance taking in the tennis courts, swimming pool, and skateboard ramps.

"It started out as a community center, but it's so much more now." He pointed to Jax, who was gardening with a group of kids, then to Olivia, who was making a banner with another group. He spotted Ving and one of the therapy dogs off in the distance. They were playing catch with a group of teens. The two exchanged a wave.

"A lot of the kids that hang out here are latchkey kids, who deep down are looking for guidance. They think of it as nothing more than a community center where they can swim and play games. Some of the other kids have been put here by me because everyone deserves a second chance."

They walked past the pool, where Jacob was giving lessons. They exchanged a wave and Luke continued, "The men and women who hang out here are counselors." He gave her a sly grin. "The kids just don't know it. They involve them in activities, which actually teach moral intelligence. They lead by example, and show how their actions affect others, which is why on weekends members from the veterans' hospital are brought in. The kids aren't forced to play games with them, but eventually they all do. Those men are funny, and their stories have such deeper meaning. The kids learn about their war experiences, their lives, their loves and their losses. Believe it or not, it has a huge effect on the kids."

"I believe it." She went quiet for a moment, her shoes tapping on the cement walkway as they rounded the building, then she asked, "Did you start the program?"

"Along with my buddy Shane. Want to meet him?"

She nodded. "Was he a soldier?"

"Yeah, for awhile, then he went back to school and got a psychology degree. He and his wife, Callie, as well as their twelve-year-old daughter, Amber, all spend their weekends here." He pointed to the distance, to where Callie and Amber were playing horseshoes with a few kids. "There they are over there."

"What a great family. Shane sounds like a terrific guy."

"He is."

She nudged him. "So are you."

While he wanted to say he was sure her father wouldn't agree, he clamped his mouth shut. Now was not the time to remind her of that. Taylor had spoiled enough of his life as it was. He didn't want him invading his thoughts and ruining this afternoon for Emery, because it was clear that having Jeremy here was important to her, which somehow made it important to him.

"So you sent Trent here because he needed guidance."

It was a statement, not a question, but he once again found himself saying, "Yeah, I like to give second chances."

She gave him a quizzical look, opened her mouth like she was about to say something but then shut it again when he gestured with a nod.

"Speak of the devil."

Just then Shane and Trent exited through the center's back entrance. They were in deep conversation and at first didn't see Luke and Emery approaching.

"Hey, how's it going?" Luke asked.

Trent's glance darted to Luke, then to Emery. Within seconds his relaxed demeanor was gone, every muscle in his body stiffening as he slipped into punk mode. Luke got the distinct impression Trent didn't want Shane to know the real reason he was there, but Shane was well aware of it long before now. Of course, he wasn't about to out the boy in front of him. He wanted Trent and Shane to bond.

"Luke," Shane said, stepping up to him to give him a big hug. "I was just inside and met Jeremy. Frank said you brought him here to play chess."

Luke nodded. "Jeremy is Emery's brother." Shane looked at Emery and smiled.

"I hope you don't mind." She shot Luke a worried glance. "We thought he might enjoy it."

"Of course not. Everyone is welcome here." Shane held his hand out. "Clearly our friend has lost his manners," he teased. "I'm Shane Conrad." He narrowed his eyes. "You look very familiar."

"Emery Vincent," she returned, and Shane angled his head, his eyes moving over her like he was trying to place her. "You might recognize me from Taylor's Market."

Shane's back went as stiff as the cement beneath their feet as his gaze flew to Luke's. A barrage of mixed emotions moved over his face as he stood there uncomfortable, like he didn't know what to say next.

"I'm setting up security for her store," Luke explained

quickly. Then he turned his attention to Trent, who was shifting restlessly beside Shane.

"What are you two up to? Did we catch you in the middle of something?"

"No," Trent said, and while he was trying to make it look like he hated being there, Luke suspected otherwise. He caught the huge smile on the kid's face before he spotted him and Emery coming his way.

"We were just about to pull some vegetables for lunch." Shane put one hand on Trent's shoulder. "Apparently Trent has never seen a vegetable garden before."

A hint of a smile curled Trent's lips, but when he saw Luke watching him, he wiped it away.

"I'll leave you to it." Luke waved his hand toward the garden. "I'm just going to give Emery a tour, then I have to get her back to work."

Shane gave him one more questioning look, confusion and worry dancing in his eyes before he led Trent off.

"What was that all about?" Emery asked, moving a bit closer to him.

"Nothing," he said, and redirected the conversation. "You know, you need help at the market, and after a few weeks here, I think Trent will have learned a lot about right from wrong. Maybe, in exchange for groceries, he can help you stock shelves and do a little more of the heavy lifting. It would give him a way to help his family and a sense of pride."

Her eyes lit. "I never thought...that's actually a great idea."

"Yeah?" he asked, almost surprised that she'd hire a kid who'd stolen from her store. But then again she'd hired Luke and asked him to stay on when she found out who he was. He shook his head, because honest to God, she confused the hell out of him.

Luke spent the next hour showing her around and

explaining all the programs. What he didn't tell her was who Shane really was, and why he spent all his spare time giving back to the community and trying to help those less fortunate.

By the time they made it back to Jeremy, he had a crowd gathered around, and the smile that lit Emery's face, warmed Luke inside.

"Maybe someday we can bring him to the store and he can check out surveillance van with me. I bet he'd love that."

She turned to him, and a strange, almost confused look moved over her face. "Why would you do that?"

He shrugged. "Why not?"

"I just...I guess I'm not sure what's in it for you?"

Now it was his turn to be confused. "Why does there have to be something in it for me?"

"I...I just..."

Jeremy started clapping and jumped up, pulling their attention to him. Frank laughed out loud, and said, "That's it. You beat me six games in a row!"

"I always win," Jeremy said. He turned to Emery. "Em, tell them. I always win."

She stepped up to her brother. "That's right, Jeremy. You always win." She took his hand in hers. "We're going to go now." When Jeremy frowned and looked distressed, Emery said, "I think Frank needs to rest."

Picking up on the cues, Frank rubbed his hand over his balding head and yawned. "Yeah, Jeremy. I need to rest now, but you come back and see me again soon. I'm going to practice and next time I'm going to win."

Jeremy clapped harder. "Okay, Frank. I'll come back. But I always win."

Emery began leading Jeremy toward the doors, and Luke leaned into Frank. "Thanks," he said. "I really appreciate you spending time with him."

"He's a great boy." He gave Luke a wink. "And his sister is pretty hot too."

"Hey," Luke said, "eyes to yourself."

"I might be old, but I'm not dead," Frank shot back. Luke laughed, and Frank added, "You two make a nice couple. If you screw it up, send her my way, will you?"

Without bothering to tell him they weren't a couple, Luke shook his head and followed behind Emery.

It was late afternoon by the time they left. After dropping Jeremy off, he headed to his place to take care of Rex. As he pulled into his driveway, he noticed Emery was unusually quiet.

"Everything okay?"

"Yeah. I was just thinking about all you do. You're kind of..."

She paused like she was searching for the right word, so he jumped in to help her. "Incredible, sexy, outstanding in bed..."

She grinned. "Yeah, but I was thinking more along the line of giving."

He was about to tell her exactly what he'd like to *give* her when her stomach grumbled.

She laughed and he reached over Rex to run her hair through his fingers. The second he touched her, electricity sparked between them. Even Rex seemed to notice. He whined, lowered his head and placed his palm over his eyes.

Something flitted across her face, something that looked like desire, want...*need*. She bit down on her lower lip, and his eyes went to her mouth. So lush, so perfect, so sexy when it was wrapped around his cock. His eyes moved back to hers and hunger clawed at his insides.

"Maybe before you take me back, we can go inside and you can introduce me to your culinary skills."

"You want to come in?"

"Yeah," she said, her voice a soft, seductive whisper.

"Just so you know, Emery. If you come in there are other skills I'm going to introduce you to first."

"Just so you know, Luke. I was counting on you saying that."

7

The look on Luke's face was intense as he and Rex circled the truck. His hand closed over hers, and her entire body trembled in response. He gripped her tight and without speaking, led her up the stairs to the apartment. Unlocking it quickly, he let Rex go and hauled her inside.

Eyes fixed on her, he dragged her against him, his hard cock pressing firmly, intently against her stomach. Emery stood there breathless, but not from the three flights of stairs they'd just climbed. No, she could barely draw in air because of the hungry way Luke was looking at her. Like if he didn't strip her down and push inside her within the next two seconds, he was going to go off like a grenade.

The air conditioning hit them and he wiped the back of his hand over his forehead before backing her up until she was pressed against the wall.

She loved his passion, the way he turned all his focus on her when they were about to get naked together. He reached over his shoulders and tugged off his T-shirt, and when she caught his scent her entire body went up in flames.

She put her hands on his body and slid them over his bare skin. He threw his head back, a sound rumbling in his throat as he briefly closed his eyes.

She wet her dry lips and could feel the tension inside him. "I love touching you."

He blinked his eyes back open, and his nostrils flared as he rested his forehead against hers. In such a Luke move, he put his hands on the wall over her head, and pushed his knee between her legs.

"Emery," he said, his gaze moving over her face as sexual heat leapt between them.

"Yeah."

"I'm going to fuck you so hard." His cock jumped against her stomach, and her pussy clenched and moistened with need. "I'm going to take you to my bed and make you come with my mouth, and then my fingers. And just when you think you can't come anymore, I'm going to pull you down onto my cock and fuck you until you scream out my name. I promise you that."

"Oh, God," was all she could manage to say.

"Tell me you want that, sunshine." His breath came harder, labored, washing over her face and arousing her even more. "Tell me you need it as much as I do."

Heat curled through her. "I do," she whispered and the next thing she knew his lips were claiming hers, his hot kisses burning her mouth and searing her between the legs.

She could barely catch her breath when his hands were all over her, pushing, pulling and ripping at her clothes. She in turn tore at his jeans. She unhooked the button and drew down the zipper then put her hand inside. The hard length of his cock felt so good in her palm, and all she could think about was putting him in her mouth again.

Luke shoved his hands into her pants, and when he swiped her clit, she sagged against the wall, her hand working faster over his cock as she closed her eyes against the flood of heat. Her legs went weak, and he must have sensed it. The next thing she knew she was in his arms, her legs wrapped around his back.

Without his mouth ever leaving hers, he carried her to his bedroom, sitting himself onto the edge of his unmade bed. He deepened the kiss, his tongue devouring her as he tore at her shirt. Her buttons popped and scattered to the floor, but she didn't care about the damage. No, all she cared about was having his cock inside her again.

He pushed her shirt off her shoulders and unhooked her bra. He gave a low, tortured moan as he took one nipple into his mouth. Her body grew hotter, needier.

In a movement that was so quick it took her by surprise, not to mention a little rough, he flipped her over until she was flat on her stomach in the middle of the mattress. He climbed over her, pushing her hair away from her shoulders and kissing the side of her neck. His cock pressed against her ass and she raised it slightly, rubbing up against him.

He growled and smacked her ass. "Cut it out or I'll lose it."

A thrill moved through her. Not only did she love him like this, no one had ever slapped her ass before, and it secretly excited her.

He kissed a path down her back, running his hands over her quivering flesh. When he reached the small of her back, he gripped the top of her jeans and said, "Lift."

She inched her ass up and he pulled her pants and panties to her knees, then he pulled her shoes off and nudged her to lift her calves. She settled back on the mattress and he peeled them the rest of the way down her legs, carelessly tossing them on the floor.

"Christ," he murmured, his hands running up her thighs to widen them.

She'd never been flat out on a bed with her ass up to a man before. But she loved the way he wanted her, the way she was trying new, naughty things with him.

The second his tongue touched her inner thigh she moaned and wiggled slightly. Luke grabbed a pillow and shoved it under her hips, lifting her ass even more.

His fingers followed his tongue, and a strangled cry lodged in her throat.

"Luke," she cried out, needing him to touch the hungry spot between her legs before she went up in a ball of flames. She ached for him, craved his touch in ways she shouldn't, ways that actually frightened her.

"Open wider," he commanded.

She spread her legs, and felt his hot breath on her pussy as he exhaled slowly. Her body grew tight, her pussy clenching in anticipation.

"So damn perfect," he said. "So wet and ready for me."

He slid up her leg, and kissed her ass cheeks as his fingers slipped between her thighs. Through his jeans his cock pressed against the back of her leg as he dipped inside her pussy. She lifted her hips, wanting his fingers deeper, harder.

"Stop," he said, giving her ass another slap.

A moan caught in her throat, her skin burning from the whack, and she bit down on her lip to fight the urge to squirm again, even though she *wanted* another slap.

"Oh you like that do you?" he said, and while she couldn't see him, she just knew he was grinning at her. He gave her another little slap, like he was testing her, and this time there was no stifling the moan in her throat.

He pulled in a breath, his fingers running over her cheeks to soothe the sting left behind. His voice sounded harsh, labored when he said, "Sunshine, you have no idea what you're doing to me right now."

Oh but she did know. The way his cock was thickening

against her leg told her everything she needed to know—he was just as crazed as she was.

He pushed another finger into her and she gripped his bedsheets, pulling them to her face. She breathed in his scent, losing herself in the sensations between her legs as he drove in and out of her.

His fingers plunged deeper, circling the hot bundle of nerves that had her toes curling. She gave a whimper as her entire body burned hotter than it ever had before. He picked up the pace, like he knew just what she needed to reach her peak. She was close, so damn close.

"Get on your knees and lift your ass higher, baby."

As soon as she did, her muscles tightened around his fingers, making her feel so gloriously full. Still pumping deep, he swiped her clit and the second he did she climaxed all over him.

"Luke," she cried out, unable to believe how hard her muscles were spasming, how much liquid heat was dripping down her legs. He kept his fingers inside her as she rode out each delicious wave of her orgasm and when she finally stopped clenching down on them, he flipped her onto her back and tossed the pillow away. She caught the raw lust in his eyes before he buried himself between her legs, licking her, slowly at first, and avoiding her sensitive clit. But in no time at all desire once again began pulling at her. The guy was turning her into some sort of nymphomaniac.

He licked her hard, his tongue picking up speed as it slashed against her, stroking fast and deep. When he finally brushed the soft tip over her clit, she gripped his head and lifted her hips from the bed, holding him there.

"Yes," she hissed, bucking against him shamelessly. Truthfully, she wasn't a prude in bed, but she'd never been this wild, this uninhibited. Luke brought out a different side of her.

His fingers bit into her thighs and using only his mouth

he brought her to orgasm again. As she came in his mouth, some small working brain cell told her so far he was true to his words. He'd made her come with his fingers and his mouth. Her heart leapt, because she remembered what else he promised her—to make her come with his cock.

He finished lapping her juices, and slid off her. He flattened himself on the bed beside her. "Come here," he said.

She rolled onto him and he gripped her hip, urging her upward. "I want to see you when you come this time."

As she straddled him, the muscles along his jaw rippled and he warned, "Don't move." Balancing her on her knees, his hard cock pointed upward, so close to her opening, he reached to his nightstand and grabbed a condom. Working between her legs, he rolled it on and she suspected he was purposely nudging her clit in some teasing, torturous attempt to drive her insane.

"Oh, God," she cried out when she caught his grin. Didn't he know how close she was to losing her damn mind?

His smile fell as he ran his hands over her breasts, then grabbed her hands to place them on her body. She met his glance as she cupped both breasts, which felt so hot and heavy in her palms, and when she saw heat flitting across his face, she wet her thumb and rubbed it over her nipple.

Two could play his game.

"Oh, fuck," he growled, his hands going to her hips. With little finesse and much greed, he pulled her down onto his cock, driving into her so hard and deep, her womb clenched. Her body trembled, loving the length of him, the depth of penetration this position gave them.

He gripped her hips and powered his upward. She moved with him, meeting each thrust and sinking back down onto his hard shaft.

One hand left her hips and cupped her face. She leaned

into his touch as the scent of their lovemaking filled the room.

"So good," he murmured. "So fucking good."

They pounded against each other, and in no time at all sweat broke on Luke's forehead. He began panting, his fingers digging into her hard enough to leave bruises. But she wanted to be bruised by him, wanted to remember every minute of this, because she truthfully had no idea when this wild affair would come to an end. She only knew it would.

Pushing that last thought aside, she squeezed her nipples, and rode him harder.

He lifted her until only his crown remained inside then he pulled her down, taking her breath away with each powerful thrust. She gasped for air, and launched herself back down onto his beautiful cock.

Her nerves sizzled, and blood pooled between her legs as he continued to fill her.

"You're going to come for me again, sunshine," Luke said, his voice rough with need and lust and something else, something she couldn't quite identify. She put her hand between her legs and stroked her clit.

"Ah, Jesus, you're going to be the death of me, girl."

Her body flared hot, and once again she climaxed, just like he said she would. As juices poured from her, Luke held her gaze, and it was all she could do not to sob from the pleasure.

"That's it," he said through clenched teeth, like it was taking every ounce of strength he had to hang on. "You're so beautiful when you come."

A second later something in his expression changed, some deeper need backlighting his pewter eyes. He pulled her off his cock and once again flipped her over until she was lying facedown on the mattress.

He widened her legs and moved in between them, and

when she felt his hands on her backside, one finger rubbing between her cheeks, uncertainty moved through her.

She looked over her shoulders and her heart nearly stopped at the way he was looking at her. His muscles were tense, his eyes severe and penetrating as they moved over her face.

"Luke," she questioned.

"I need to take you. Everywhere." His finger dipped inside her ass cheeks, and when he touched her puckered opening she clenched. "I need to have all of you."

She hesitated, never having done anything like this before. But there was no denying that she was already in over her head with him, doing things she shouldn't be doing. Truthfully, when she was with Luke it felt like she was skydiving without a parachute. It was both exciting and terrifying.

"I'm guessing you haven't been taken this way before," he began, urgency and emotion in his voice as he tucked her bottom up against him. "If you say no, I'll stop."

"Luke," she said, putting a pillow beneath her as she warmed to the idea. "I want you to have all of me."

He leaned over her and pressed his chest to her back, his mouth going to her neck. His hands moved over her sides, and she was almost certain they were trembling. He grabbed something from his nightstand, and a second later she felt cool liquid between her cheeks.

One finger entered her, and he gently moved it in and out, letting her get used to the new sensations. For the first time Luke was being gentle with her, taking his time despite the fact that she could sense his restraint as he prepared her. In that moment everything inside her went out to him. She loved that he was going slow, wanting to do this right for her.

He stretched her open and slipped another finger in. He leaned over her and put his mouth near her ear. His breath was hot, ragged on her neck when he whispered, "If it hurts, tell me and I'll stop."

He pulled his fingers out and positioned his cock. His crown breached her opening and she gripped the sheets. Luke's hands closed over hers and held her tight. He remained still, giving her time to adjust.

"You okay, sunshine?" he asked.

"Yes," she whispered.

"I can keep going?" He ran his hands along her sides, sweeping the outer edge of her breasts. His touch was commanding, yet soft, each furtive brush triggering a craving inside her unlike anything she'd ever before experienced. God she wanted this, wanted him.

She nodded and wiggled against him, encouraging him to take her...everywhere.

He leaned back over her, his hands gripping hers once again. "Fuck, baby, don't do that."

She grinned, loving the way he was losing it. As he fell over her, his weight pressing her into the mattress, the sheets felt rough against her breasts. She moved against the linen, stimulating her taut nipples.

"Fuck." He let go of her hand, and gave her a smack on the side of her ass. "Cut it out," he growled and pushed another inch inside.

It stung at first, but as soon as she relaxed her ringed muscles he drove a little deeper. His growl curled around her and then in one fluid movement he was inside her. Moisture sealed their bodies as one and his breathing turned ragged against her ear.

"You okay?" he asked.

She moved against him, answering his question. He pressed a kiss to her neck before he began pumping into her, the lubricant making it easy for him to slide in and out. His tension mounted and she knew he was teetering on the edge as he settled his hands on her hips. Wanting to make this even better for him, she went up on her knees. He followed her up, and she could feel a shudder overtake him.

"I'm there baby. You got me right fucking there."

She pushed against him, and he leaned down and slipped a hand around her waist, pulling her impossibly closer.

Her breath hitched as he plunged hungrily, moving urgently over her body as he chased his own orgasm. His cock jolted inside her. He pounded once, twice, then stilled inside her. He growled deep and a moment later, she felt that first sweet pulse of his release. He fell over her and his lashes brushed her flesh as he bit down on her shoulder, not hard enough to break skin, but definitely hard enough to leave his mark.

"Emery," he whispered into her ear, and everything in the way her name rolled of his tongue brought them to an even deeper level of intimacy.

Still trying to catch her breath, she couldn't answer him. All she could do was whimper. Luke pulled out of her and then flipped her over. Gray eyes full of tender concern moved over her.

"Hey," he said. "You okay?"

She touched his cheek and when she smiled the worry left his eyes.

He raked his fingers through her hair. "I thought I hurt you." His fingers trailed over her arm and he shifted closer. As he pressed against her, it occurred to her that giving herself to him like this felt more intimate than anything they'd ever done. He pressed a kiss to her mouth and a riot of emotions rushed through her, but she quickly tamped them down.

He pulled her toward him, and gave her a light whack on the ass. "Come on." Jumping from the bed, he reached for her hand.

"Can we at least wait until my legs stop shaking?"

He laughed and scooped her up.

"Where are you taking me?" she asked.

"Shower, then I'm going to introduce you to some of my culinary skills."

She wrapped her arms around his neck and held on as he carried her down the narrow hall. They reached his small bathroom and he set her on the counter as he adjusted the spray. A moment later they were both inside, taking turns to wash each other's bodies. Luke took extra care between her legs, touching her with gentle hands.

She looked at the man who was taking such good care of her and knew there was so much more to him than met the eye. She saw a side of him today that touched something deep inside her. And the way he was with Jeremy, going out of his way to take him to the compound and the center, was the kindest sweetest thing anyone had ever done for her.

She looked at him as he soaped her up, taking in his rugged features, the tattoos on his lethal body, the scars on his flesh—the mouth that kissed her with intense passion. Good God, if she wasn't careful she could easily fall for him. But she knew better than to expect more and she could only imagine what her father would say if he ever found out his daughter was having an affair with the guy he'd sent to juvie. The more she thought about that, the more she realized that Luke didn't seem like the kind of guy to steal. Then again, maybe, like Trent, he had a reason. Maybe he needed the food to help feed his family. But did that make it right? An uneasy feeling formed in her stomach. Even still, if he was trying to feed his family, was putting him in juvie for the rest of his teenage years the right thing to do?

I believe in second chances.

As she thought about the words she'd heard from him more than once, she ran her soapy fingers over his stomach, and even though she knew it wasn't wise, she couldn't help but want to know more.

"Luke."

"Yeah."

"Who was the girl going into the coffee shop?" His hand closed over hers and tightened. When he didn't answer, she asked, "Was it your sister?"

He nodded.

"She's very pretty."

Luke shifted toward the spray, turning his body slightly away from hers. "She looks like our mother."

"You mother must be beautiful."

"She was."

Was?

"Oh, I'm sorry."

He dunked his head under the spray and it poured down his face. "It was a long time ago."

"I lost my mom too."

"I know."

"You do?"

"Yeah."

Luke grabbed her and turned her around so the spray washed the rest of the soap from her body. "What about your dad? Is he still alive?" she asked.

At the mention of his dad, his entire body went rigid, and she knew she'd hit a sore spot.

"No, he's gone too."

"So it's just you and your sister."

Luke reached behind her and turned off the water. "Yeah, but Allison and I don't really speak."

She listened to the sound of his throat working as he swallowed, and knew there was way more going on than he was telling her. "That's kind of sad."

He grabbed a towel from his rack and wrapped it around her, then tied one at his waist. "It is what it is."

"When did you two stop speaking?" she pressed as she followed him back to his bedroom.

At the door he stopped and turned to her. "I don't really think we should do this, okay?"

"Why? Why does it upset you so much to talk about her?"

He braced his hands on the top of the doorframe, and exhaled slowly. "Because I pushed her out of my life and hurt her."

"Oh," she said for lack of anything else. "I'm sorry."

He just stood there for a moment, his eyes focused on something over her shoulders, like he was a million miles away. "A girl needs her father," he whispered and she wondered if he even knew he'd spoken out loud. She took in the tension in his body, the muscles rippling along his jaw.

"I'm not sure what happened, Luke, but from what I know about you, you're a guy to give second chances and I just bet your sister is too."

Something in him seemed to give, break, and the vulnerability she caught on his face nearly took the wind right out of her.

He put his hands on her shoulders. "But what if she's not. What if she looks me in the face and tells me to leave her alone." He gave a hard shake of his head. "I couldn't handle that, Emery. I just couldn't. I saw that hurt look once—I goddamn well put it on her face—and I can't see it again." He swallowed, hard, then continued, "I'm better off keeping my distance and watching her from afar."

"Oh, Luke. I'm so sorry."

His arms wrapped around her and he held her so tight she could barely draw air. Realizing she was probably seeing a side of him that he'd never shown another, and how hard that must be for him, she couldn't help but want to do something to help him mend his relationship with his sister. But the last thing she wanted to do was overstep boundaries in a sex-only affair.

Deciding it was time to change the subject, because she'd clearly pushed him too far, she said, "So about those culinary skills. If they're anything like your bedroom skills, then I guess I'm in for a real treat." She reached down and gave him a whack on the ass.

He pulled back and looked at her. Understanding arced between them when their eyes met, and he gave her a small grateful smile.

Her towel slipped and his mood instantly changed. "I'm not sure we're going to make it to the kitchen anytime soon, sunshine."

"If I don't get to work, I could get fired. My boss is a real dragon."

"Really." He dipped his head, his mouth inches from hers. "I bet I could sweet talk her into letting you stay and play a little longer. In fact, I bet there are a lot of things I could talk her into doing."

She laughed. "Of that I have no doubt. So far you've gotten your way with her. But I really do need to go." She planted her hands on her hips, and frowned. "And I'm wondering what I'm supposed to wear."

His brow furrowed. "What do you mean?"

"You ripped the buttons off my blouse, remember?"

He gave her a sheepish look. "Oh, right." Heat moved into his eyes like he was remembering every last detail, and he brushed her nipples through the cotton towel.

"Luke," she said, moaning. "You're turning me into a nymphomaniac."

He inched the towel down and wrapped his hot mouth around one hard nub. "There are worse things you could be," he said after a thorough taste.

"Oh yeah, like what?" she asked, as her hands went to his shoulders. She touched him lightly and he trembled.

"Oh, like you could be one of those unhappy guards at Buckingham Palace." His mouth curved. "Or better yet, a sex slave...mine to do with as I please."

She leaned into him, losing herself in his touch all over again. "I think I already am that." She heard Rex's nails on the floor, and the sound helped pull her back.

"You're a bad influence." Even though her pussy was clenching, she shoved him through the door and went in search of her clothes. She pulled on her panties, jeans and bra and listened to Luke shuffle into his own clothes. When she turned back to him he handed her one of his T-shirts.

"Will this work for now?"

She pulled it on and Luke's eyes dropped to her chest. "What is it about a girl in a guy's shirt that is so sexy." He walked toward her. "Jesus Christ. We're never going to get out of here."

His mouth found hers and he kissed her deeply. "One more time, sunshine. I'll make it fast, then I'll make you something to eat and take you back to work before your boss ever finds out you're gone."

His cock pressed against her midriff and she sagged against him. There was just no way she could ignore the heat between them. Maybe one more time would finally sate her need for him. "Well when you put it like that."

He unhooked her button and quickly dragged her pants down her legs and discarded them. Once he had her half naked, he unzipped and pulled out his cock, not bothering to remove their shirts or take his pants off all the way. He quickly sheathed himself, backed her up against his wall, lifted her onto his hips and drove into her.

"Ah, Jesus," he growled, his cock throbbing so hard inside her. "I just can't enough of you."

He fucked her hard against the wall, but as he did, she was suddenly sure that no matter how many times he took her nothing could sate the restless ache between her thighs. No man fucked like Luke. With such passion, energy and vigor. He was simply incredible and she had no idea how she could ever be with another man after him.

"Luke," she cried out, clawing at the back of his shirt as he drove deep. The air around them grew heavy, both of them panting hard as the tension mounted. He grunted, and brushed his pelvis over her clit, pushing her over the edge in record time.

"Oh, God," she cried out as she creamed all over his cock.

He slammed her against the wall, and stilled as the pictures rattled. "Fuck," he bit out as he buried his mouth in the hollow of her neck and released inside her.

A strange, strangled noise crawled out of her throat and she couldn't help but laugh. This was so crazy, so insane.

"What?" he asked through labored breaths.

"That was…"

"I know," he said in a teasing voice. "I was awesome." He let her legs slide down his and when she hit the floor, he gave her ass a whack and said, "Now no more talk about being my sex slave or we'll seriously never get out of here."

She tugged her jeans back on as he tucked his cock in, and as she looked at him, and then herself, it occurred to her that they both had that well-fucked look about them. She wondered if anyone else would pick up on that.

"Let's eat. I'm starving. Are you ready for the Phillips special?"

She smiled. "I thought I just had that."

"That was just the sampler," he teased in return.

They left the bedroom, and after taking care of Rex, Luke met her in his small kitchen. He grabbed a few things from his fridge and like a typical guy—even though she was learning he was anything but—he whipped up scrambled eggs and toast. But she had to admit, it was the best afternoon meal she'd ever tasted. Probably because she didn't have to make it herself and she was starved from all the great sex.

A half hour later they were on his bike. He stopped at her place so she could change her top, then he took her to the market.

She couldn't seem to wipe the silly, sex-sated grin off her face as he parked his bike and followed her in to the store, insisting he had to check on a few things. He went one way while she went to her office to go over last week's numbers and this week's deliveries and work schedules.

She stopped midstride when she saw a bouquet of flowers on her desk. Her heart leapt, and she instantly assumed Luke had sent them. Heavy footsteps heralded his approach and when she turned and caught the hard look on Luke's face, her smile fell.

"Who are they from?" he asked, his jaw clenched tight.

"Oh, I thought..." Her glance went from Luke, to the flowers, back to Luke again. She walked across the room and grabbed the card.

"Let me guess. Lane?"

She looked up at him, and once again she caught that dark haunted look in his eyes as he stared down at her.

8

"You okay, boss man?" Colt asked as Luke stared at the surveillance cameras from inside the van. He looked over last night's records, noting that the back service door had been opened around midnight. The system wasn't set up to take snapshots yet, but he wondered if it was a glitch in the wiring or if Emery had come back to the store after closing up.

"Yeah," he said. "I just need to set up the camera on the back door right away." He shot Colt a glance. "Did you finish wiring the monitors in Emery's office?"

Just saying her name out loud had the strangest effect on him. *Emery.* Sweet Emery who'd let him do all kinds of wild things to her every night for the last week. Emery who'd opened her body to him, trusting him in a way she'd never trusted another. He had no idea why that was so important to him, or why he desperately needed to take her...everywhere. All he knew was that he had to. In the heat of the moment last weekend, leaving his mark on her had become more important than breathing. Then after sex he turned around and told her about his sister. What the hell? Besides with a couple of his closest comrades he never opened up to anyone about Allison.

"Yup, everything should be set to go," Colt said.

Luke nodded, and turned back to his monitors. His glance went to Emery as she walked past one of the cameras and a rush of sexual energy hit him hard. She was so goddamn sexy, it damn near killed him to see her and not be able to touch her. After their wild weekend in bed, he's spent just about every night with her, despite the flowers he'd found on her desk. Flowers that were like a kick in the balls and reminded him that not only should he not be fucking her, he shouldn't be sharing past hurts. They were different people who had no future together, and if he knew what was good for him, he would be backing the hell off.

But damned if his cock cared anything about that.

For some strange reason, it touched him on a deeper level when she opened up to him about her brother. He suspected it was a difficult thing for her to do. And in turn he found himself bringing her and her brother into his world where he showed them the dog training compound and the community center.

One thing he was happy about doing, however, was putting a stop to her delivering bread to the homeless at night and instead setting up a meeting at the end of the day through the back service doors.

He glanced at his watch. In a few short hours, he'd be checking out for the weekend, and damned if he didn't want to go to Sky Bar for a couple of cold ones and to get his head on straight where Emery was concerned. But first he needed to talk to her about the back door and find out if she was at the market after hours.

She walked by again, and his cock twitched. There was no denying that he wanted her again. In fact, he wanted to walk into her office, bend her over her desk and take her good and fucking hard right now.

He exited the van and walked inside. Moving with purpose, he made his way back to her office and found her frowning as she looked over data on her computer. She glanced up, like she sensed his presence.

"Luke," she said, sounding breathless.

He sat across from her. "I wanted to talk to you about your service door."

"Okay."

"After I left your place last night, did you come here?"

She shook her head, worry moving into her eyes. "No, why?"

"Does anyone have a key to the market?"

She nodded. "Just me and my father."

"Would he have any reason to be here at midnight?"

She looked down, her face thoughtful, then she said, "Not that I know of. The running of the business is left to me. I can't see any reason why he'd be here. I can check in with him if you want."

A very uneasy feeling moved into Luke's gut. Something just wasn't sitting right with him. "No, that's okay, don't worry him. Maybe there is a glitch in the wiring. I'll check it out." He looked at her face, and when he saw real concern he said, "What?"

"I don't know." She looked back at her laptop screen. "I've been running numbers and found something odd. With the new inventory tracking system you set up, there seems to be some very expensive deli meats going missing." She pointed to something on her computer, and he climbed from his chair, crossed the desk and leaned over her. "I recently received an order of very expensive prosciutto ham. We have them shipped in from Italy, and a twenty-pound package has just gone missing." She shrugged and held her hands up. "Who would walk out of here with a ham that size?"

Luke scrubbed his chin. "I don't know, but believe me, in this business I've heard of stranger things walking out the door." He considered it for a moment, and decided a trip to the nearest pawnshop was in order. He'd learned over the years that people traded the strangest things for coin. But he couldn't think about that right now, not when he was standing so close to Emery and she smelled so fucking good.

He was pretty sure he was going into Emery withdrawal, even though he'd fucked her two times last night. He'd almost considered spending the night so he could wake up and take her again this morning. But he wasn't about to spend the night with her, because this wasn't a relationship and that could only complicate things. And he guessed it gave him some measure of comfort to know that she wasn't looking for anything more either. At least they both knew what to expect, and what not to. He spun her chair around to face him, and leaned closer, his body aching for her.

He heard her breathing change, and her body went tight. "Luke," she whispered, her big blue eyes searching his face. "Here?"

Knowing he was fighting a losing battle, and unable to bank his desires around her, he exhaled slowly and brushed his thumb over her mouth. She was like drug. One taste and he was addicted. As the air around them charged, he lowered his voice. "I haven't been able to stop thinking about you since I left your bed last night," he admitted.

"Me neither," she said, and swiped her tongue over her bottom lip. She glanced around his shoulders, blinking nervously. "The staff, your crew?"

With blood leaving his brain in a whoosh, he could no longer think with clarity, or make sane rational decisions. Especially when it came to her. Even though it was risky and inappropriate to get naked with her in the middle of the afternoon in her office, he inched back and kicked her door closed.

"I don't care about your staff or my crew. All I care about is being inside you again."

She exhaled quickly and Luke lifted her from her chair. His lips found hers and he kissed her like a man starved for more than just sex.

Their tongues tangled and she pushed against him, rubbing herself over his thigh just the way he liked, and letting him know she was just as desperate to have him inside her as he was to be there. Her hands tangled in his hair and her soft moan of surrender had to be about the sexiest thing he'd ever heard. Her chest heaved, and he could feel her nipples harden against him.

He deepened the kiss, reveling in the flavor of her mouth. God, she tasted so sweet, like honey and cinnamon, and... peanut butter. He broke the kiss and she stared up at him, confusion in her eyes. Her hand went to his cheek and her confusion changed to concern.

"Are you okay?" Panic spread across her face when he started wheezing.

"Shit, Emery," he choked out. "Did you eat peanut butter?"

She nodded, shaky hands waving to the crumbs on a piece of paper towel. "I was busy so I just made a peanut butter sandwich for lunch and ate it at my desk." She started wrapping her apron around her hand. "Oh, God, you're allergic aren't you?"

"Van," he managed to get out as he dropped down into her chair. "EpiPen."

She ran from the office and Luke tried to calm himself as his throat began to close up. He gasped for breath, and gripped the sides of the chair as the room began to spin. In no time at all Emery came running back. She held the pen out to him.

"Tell me what to do?"

He grabbed it from her, flipped open the tube and slid the pen from the case. He jammed the needle into his thigh through his jeans, and pumped himself full of epinephrine. Time seemed to stand still as he waited, and a minute later, the swelling started to go down, making breathing a little easier, but he knew, because his allergy was so severe, he'd have to take a trip to the ER.

Both Colt and Tanner came running in.

"Shit," Colt said, gripping his hat when he saw Luke sitting there.

"You okay, man?" Tanner asked. "Christ, your lips are blue."

"I will be," he said around a thick tongue. "But I need to get to the hospital."

Emery took the needle and case from him and placed them on her desk. "I'm coming with you." She darted to the safe. Despite the fact that all three could see her punch in the combo—something he'd have to talk to her about, when his tongue wasn't three sizes too big—she opened it and pulled out her purse.

Colt and Tanner hoisted him up and helped him out to the van. As they passed the cash register, Emery gave instructions to the new assistant manager, Tami, to lock up at closing time, then hurried to the van. She sat across from Luke, their knees touching.

She leaned in and grabbed his hand. "I didn't know."

"I probably should have told you." He tried to smile, but when Emery worked to bite back a grin, he knew he was likely channeling the Grinch. "I guess I thought Matt was the only one who still ate peanut butter."

"Matt?"

"Matt James. A friend of mine. He eats peanut butter from the jar, just like he did when we were twelve."

She laughed. "Sounds like Matt and I would get along just fine." She bumped up against him when Tanner took the corner too fast. Colt looked back to check on him. Emery squeezed his hand. "And you sound like you should stop talking." She grabbed a tissue from her apron pocket and wiped his mouth. "You're drooling."

"You okay, boss man?" Colt asked.

"Right now I have a better chance of dying from Tanner's driving than from the peanut butter."

Tanner laughed, and adjusted his ball cap. "He's going to be fine. He's back to being a hard-ass."

Luke rolled his eyes. "Tanner and his thing for asses," he said, and Colt laughed with him. Emery however, wasn't laughing at all. In fact she was nibbling her bottom lip like she was remembering their afternoon together in bed—when he put his mark on her.

"Jesus, Emery. Cut it out," he growled scratching at the red welts breaking out on his arms.

She crinkled her nose, and brushed his hand away to prevent him from rubbing. "Sorry, I couldn't help myself. Besides," she whispered. "It might take your mind off how itchy you are."

"Except thinking about that afternoon is making me swell...in other places." She fell into him again, and her scent washed over him. His cock twitched and he adjusted his pants. "And all this swelling is going to confuse the doctors."

She gave him a playful, yet seductive look and leaned closer. "The doctors can deal with the throat swelling, I'll deal with the rest."

He dropped his head into his hand. "Jesus. What am I going to do with you?"

"We're here," Colt said, and the van came to an abrupt halt. Colt was out the door before Tanner had it in park, and he slid the side door open. Emery hopped out as Colt reached for Luke.

"I'm good," Luke said, but leaned on Colt anyway. He walked into the emergency room with both men flanking him, and the second the duty nurse looked at his face she brought him right in. Within minutes they took his vitals and had him hooked up to an IV with Benadryl. Once he was being tended to and knew he was going to be there for hours, he sent Colt and Tanner home, telling them to take the rest of the afternoon off. Emery insisted on staying with him, and at first he was going to complain, but then shut his mouth because he liked having her there. Only problem was, they were in a room with a bed, and well...that had him swelling all over again.

Emery dashed to the gift shop and purchased a deck of cards. While he wanted to play strip poker, and told her how useful a swollen tongue would come in, she chose rummy and teased him for having a one-track mind, which he did. The afternoon went by in a blur of nurses, tests and IV drips, and soon enough night was upon them.

It was well after dinner when the doctor came to check on him and by then the itching had stopped and his tongue had returned to normal. Emery left the room to give them some privacy.

The doctor flipped the pages on his chart while a nurse took his blood pressure, which also had finally returned to normal.

"Looks like you're good to go," the doctor said, and the nurse went ahead and started to remove his IV. As she worked she went over the measures to protect himself from having such a reaction. Luke simply nodded and explained the situation. Christ, he hadn't had an attack since he was a child, and there was no way he could have known Emery was eating peanut butter.

The nurse then scolded him, warning that his girlfriend should know such things about him. He agreed, a girlfriend should know. But technically, Emery wasn't his girlfriend.

After the nurse left, Luke climbed from the bed and tore off the gown they made him wear.

"How are you feeling?" Emery said, peeking her head back in as he dressed.

"I'm good to go. I'm no longer symptomatic."

"I'll grab us a cab." She pulled out her phone and dialed, as Luke came up beside her. He draped one arm over her shoulder and walked out the doors with her.

When they finally made it back to the market, the lights were off and it was locked. Emery stood on the sidewalk, looking weary as she stared at her store.

He sat on his motorcycle and thought about his plans for the night, then said, "Tell me what you do for fun?"

She spun to face him. "Fun?" A laugh bubbled up in her throat. "I don't have fun." She nibbled her bottom lip. "Well, I mean, except for this time with you."

"If you could get away from the market for the weekend, what would you do?"

She went quiet, and stared at her shoes. "Honestly, it's been so long since I've done anything for myself, I'm not sure what I would do."

"How about you leave it in my hands then."

"What are you talking about?"

"You have an assistant manager now. Why don't you just let her run things this weekend, and let me spend the weekend showing you a good time." He pitched his voice low, grabbed her blouse and tugged until she was pressed up against his knee. "Let me take care of you."

Equal amounts of excitement and concern moved over her face. "The whole weekend?"

"Yeah," he said, thinking of the key he had to Caleb's cottage on the lake. It was his to use anytime and he hadn't heard any of his comrades talk about going there this weekend.

"I mean I can't just up and leave." She held her hands out at her sides. "Besides the market I have my father to think about, my brother."

"You can't not just up and leave either. You need this."

"Luke—"

"You have a cell phone. If there's an emergency, I'll bring you back."

Her eyes widened. "Where would we go?"

Luke grinned, because he knew he had her. "Get on," he said. "And I'll show you."

———

Even though she kept asking, Luke wouldn't tell her where he was taking her. He did however take her home to pack and told her to bring a bathing suit. At her townhouse she did a thorough brushing of her teeth to clear all traces of peanut butter, and solicited her neighbor to check in on Jinx. She didn't feel too bad asking, considering she'd taken care of the woman's cat a time or two when she was away on business. One thing was for certain, Emery couldn't ask her father. He'd want to know where she was going and who she was with, and she'd feel responsible to tell him. She quivered as she imagined how that scene would play out.

After locking her place, she was back on his bike with her overnight bag in tow. They made their way to his apartment to change vehicles and grab Rex. Now, with their gear and a few grocery items secured in the back of his truck and Rex in between them, Luke drove along the highway. She kept glancing out the window, trying to figure out where he was taking her.

The farther they drove from the city the more she began to question herself. She could hardly believe she was going away with him somewhere for the entire weekend, where they'd undoubtedly have wild crazy sex numerous times. What if her father needed her, her brother? What if there was an emergency at the market?

What if she fell for him?

"Emery," Luke said quietly. She turned to him, and Rex whined and put his head on her lap. "Stop worrying. Even Rex can feel your tension." He reached over Rex and grabbed her hand. "I told you everything will be fine and if anything happens I can take you back."

She nodded. "Okay. Thanks." He looked at her for a moment longer, his smile so warm and tender her heart missed a beat. Oh God, maybe she shouldn't have agreed to this, maybe she was getting in over her head with him.

When he turned back to the look out the window, she continued to watch him. As she took in the hard lines of his profile, her body warmed all over. He was so rugged, so good looking, but it wasn't just that that had her feeling more than was safe for her to feel. There was a genuine kindness about him, a deep warmth that was doing the strangest things to her. She swallowed down the lump gathering in her throat. Maybe having an affair with him wasn't her brightest idea. In fact, she knew it wasn't. Being with him physically, spending time with him like this was having an effect on her, making it harder to separate sex from emotions.

She knew from past hurts people used her to get what they wanted and discarded her afterward. But the more she got to know Luke, the more she realized he didn't seem the type to toss anyone away. Trent was a good example. He followed up with him, wanting to ensure he was getting the care he needed to make better decisions. He could have called the cops. Her father would have called them, for sure. Which once again had her wondering exactly what happened between Luke and her father all those years ago.

As much as she'd have liked to ask Luke, she knew it was a sore spot, a reason for his demon. She wondered more about his sister and why he'd pushed her out of his life. She mulled that over as Luke pulled off the highway.

He drove down a dark, back road for a few more miles, then turned down a dirt road.

"You're taking me into the woods?"

He grinned. "No worries, sunshine. I won't make you pitch a tent in the middle of the forest." He shot her a glance. "You don't look like the type who would enjoy that."

"Just for the record, I was a Girl Scout when I was young."

"So you're saying you like to camp?"

She crinkled her nose. "Ah, no not really."

His grin widened. "Well it's pure luxury where we're going."

They drove a long way down the road, and she could hear water splashing on either side of them as they went over a narrow causeway. When they reached the island, Luke slowed the truck, negotiating the tree-lined gravel road carefully. She looked to her left and then to her right, taking note of all the small cottages along the shore, and she felt a bubble of excitement well up inside of her. When she was young, and her mom was still alive, they all spent many weeks in the summer at their cottage on the lake. Her father had sold it a long time ago, but she remembered those times fondly.

She rubbed her hand over Rex's head and exhaled slowly. "Right here, Luke."

He began to brake. "What?"

"You asked me, if I could get away from the market where

I'd go." She could almost feel the tension drain out of her. "Right here." She shot him a glance. "You did good."

At the tip of the island she spotted a beautiful cottage, lit up only by the full moon overhead. He stopped his truck, and Rex jumped up and barked.

"We're here, boy," Luke said.

Emery opened her door to let Rex out and he jumped over her. "Is this yours?"

"My buddy's." He winked, grabbed his keys from the ignition and shook them. "But I have a key."

"He won't mind?"

"He's up in San Antonio working. Matt and I both have keys."

"This would be the peanut-butter-eating Matt?"

He laughed. "Yeah, come on."

Emery jumped from the truck cab and pulled her phone out. "You sure this will work way out here?"

"Are you sure you want it to?"

"Yeah, I do," she murmured.

He came around to her side and pulled her against him. "You know, sunshine, it's okay to take time for yourself. Everyone deserves a break once in a while." He dipped his head, and catching her off guard, planted a warm kiss onto her lips. She wrapped her arms around him and hugged tight. God, if he kept being so nice to her she really was going to fall for him.

"Now if you don't relax, I will tie you to my bed and make you my sex slave for the weekend."

"Right," she said, his words taking her back to when he'd flat-out told her this relationship couldn't go anywhere. It was about sex, and she'd be wise to remember that.

Luke bent down to rub Rex when he came sauntering back from his quick exploration in the trees surrounding the cottage, his tail waggling like mad. "How about a swim, boy?"

Emery reached for her bag in the back of the truck, and Luke took it from her, along with his and the bag of groceries. A floodlight flicked on as they made their way along the gravel walkway. Luke opened the front door and guided her in while Rex planted himself outside, sniffing the air and waiting for Luke to take him swimming.

Standing in the small kitchen she glanced beyond the island counter to find a huge living space with two windows overlooking the lake. A fireplace sat in the corner where the windows met, and on the opposite side of the room there were three doors and a small loft above.

"This place is gorgeous," she murmured, taking it all in.

A loud thud had her turning around. Luke dropped the bags at his feet, and pulled her to him. He ran his hands through her hair. "You're gorgeous," he said, and planted his mouth on hers again.

Her body instantly responded, heating in all the right places as he devoured her. He backed her up, out of the kitchen and into the living space. Her knees hit the sofa. Luke growled.

"I've been wanting to do this all day."

"We almost did in my office," she said.

"Yeah, I was just about ready to push your pants to your ankles, bend you over the desk and pound into you from behind."

A gasp caught in her throat, and she put her hands on his chest, and pushed him away.

He tilted his head, his eyes narrowing. "Emery?" he questioned, worry lingering in in voice.

She turned her back to him, and braced her hands on the back of the sofa as she tipped her ass up. "It's not my desk, but I think it will work." She cast him a glance over her shoulder and spread her legs in invitation. "And it's the least I could do, considering I was responsible for *all* your swelling."

A growl ripped from his lungs. "Jesus Christ, sunshine. You're killing me."

A split second later he was pressed against her, his hands circling her body. He cupped her breasts and leaned over her, pressing his chest into her back. In that instant she made the snap decision to temporarily shelve her worries and just enjoy this weekend for what it was.

His fingers worked the buttons on her blouse, and after he removed it, along with her bra, he slipped a hand inside her pants, brushing her clit and pulling open her lips to swirl his fingers through her slick heat. She pushed against him, trapping his hand against the sofa as she gyrated.

"Fuck, girl," he said into her ear, then pulled his hand free. Feeling needy, and out of control, she looked out over the moonlight ocean and listened to him shed his clothes behind her. A shiver moved through her, heat reverberating through her blood at the sound of a condom being ripped open. He made deep guttural sounds as he slid it on, and the next thing she knew he was stripping her pants from her hips and pulling them down her legs. She kicked them free, and as they both stood there naked, overlooking the water, a melee of emotions moved through her. A beautiful view, a beautiful man, doing beautiful things with her.

He settled himself over her, his chest pressed against her back as his cock slipped between her thighs. "I want you so much," he whispered, the raw ache of lust in his voice performing some mysterious alchemy on her soul as he pressed his mouth to her neck.

Her nipples tightened with arousal, as he crushed his body to hers. He reached between her legs and positioned his cock at her opening.

She moaned and tipped her ass up a bit more, providing him better access. His hands slipped up her back and he gripped her shoulders. A hard thrust later, he was deep inside her. Her sex muscles clenched and Luke mumbled heated curses behind her.

He held her tight as he pounded, driving in so hard and deep the sofa began moving across the room. But she didn't care. All she cared about was the incredible way this man made her feel.

One hand left her shoulder and slipped around her leg. He stroked her clit as he hammered into her. A whimper escaped her lips and she could feel herself growing slicker with each swipe. Soon pressure began building, coming to a peak.

"Oh, Luke," she cried out, trembling from head to toe as he swelled inside her.

She moved against his finger, seeking what her body craved and a second later her body went up in a burst of flames.

Luke fell over her back, his fingers biting into her shoulders as he joined her in release. They remained like that for a long time, like neither wanted to be the first to move. Soon he grew flaccid and pulled out. She listened as he discarded the condom but was in no hurry to move. He came back to her and pulled her against him, his mouth going to her neck.

"Has the swelling gone down?" she teased.

"Yeah, but it's only temporary."

Rex barked from outside, and Luke panted hard against her neck. His fingers moved up and down her arms. "How about we take Rex for a swim? I think he's waited long enough."

She nodded. "Good idea, and I think we could use something to cool us off. Just give me a minute to change into my suit."

"The hell we do." He spun her around and dropped a kiss onto her mouth. "And forget about the suit. It's just going to get in my way."

●9

Luke looked at the woman sitting on the dock beside him as she stared up at the stars and sipped on a glass of wine. They'd been enjoying the lake and each other for nearly twenty-four hours now, and he could already see her shoulders relaxing, the tension leaving her body. She really needed this.

They'd spent the better part of today boating, swimming, having sex everywhere and anywhere, and just doing nothing and everything, and as he looked at her now, he knew he wanted...needed...her again.

He threw his arm around her like it was the most natural thing for him to do. "Hey," he said. The moonlight spilled over her face as she smiled up at him, lighting up the flush on her cheeks, and honest to God it was cliché, but damned if she didn't take his breath away.

"You okay?" he asked.

She exhaled. "Better than okay."

He brushed his thumb along her shoulder. "This is the first time I've really seen you relaxed."

"It must be the wine."

He arched a brow. "Or all the incredible sex."

"Ego," she teased.

"Seriously, though. Do you like what you do?"

She nodded, and her eyes lit. "I actually really do love my job. I love running the market, talking with customers and bringing in special orders for them." Luke rubbed one of her shoulders, lightly massaging the muscles. She leaned into him. "Once security is in place, I'm sure I'll be back to my old self." She turned the conversation to him. "I can tell you love your job. You should have seen your face when you were explaining all the security measures to me."

"I do love it," he said. "I've been saving for a while now, and I'm getting ready to expand. There are a couple of my comrades who are discharging next month and I'm looking to buy another van."

"You did security in the military?" He nodded. "How did you get interested in that field?" As soon as the words left her mouth, her body tightened, like she was remembering his past. He could only assume her father's words were running around inside her head. But he didn't want to think about that right now. Right now he just wanted to enjoy the cottage and their time together.

Instead of answering, he drew her mouth to his, and savored the sweet wine on her tongue. His cock thickened, and just as he was about to lay her out on the wooden dock, and climb over her, the sound of a car door closing reached his ears.

"What the hell?" Another door slammed and he glanced over his shoulder. Rex jumped up, barked a couple times then sauntered toward the cottage to check things out. From where they were sitting on the dock, Luke couldn't see who'd just pulled up to the cottage, but their voices carried and he knew from the teasing jibes and easy camaraderie, it was a few of his buddies along with their wives. "Shit."

"What?" Emery followed his gaze. "Who is it?"

"A few of my friends." He listened for a moment as Matt said something crude to Caleb. Just then Sky intervened and they all laughed. Then he heard Garrett and Josh talking and he bit down hard enough to break bone.

She gave him an uneasy look. "Is this bad?"

"I didn't know they'd be coming here."

"Luke, where the hell are you?" Matt called out.

"Get your sorry ass up here," Caleb added.

"Guess they saw my truck."

"Or Rex," she added. She nudged him with her shoulder and toyed with the stem of her wine glass. "We should probably go say hello."

His stomach tightened. "I'm not sure it's a good idea."

Her eyes moved over his face. "Why?"

"I don't think you'd fit in so well with them." He paused for a moment, then added, "Just like I wouldn't fit in so well with your friends. We both know we don't run in the same circles."

"You fit in me, so that's all that matters," she said. "And I don't have to worry about you fitting in with my friends, because—" She stopped speaking abruptly, like she'd said too much, and looked away.

He read her body language and took in her discomfort. Unease gripped him as he placed a finger under her chin and turned it until their eyes met. His heart tightened as he took in the pain in her eyes, the sadness that ran deep.

He brushed his thumb over her cheek. "What are you not telling me?" he asked quietly.

"Nothing." She frowned, and tried to move away but he wouldn't let her.

"You're not going anywhere until you talk to me."

She forced a smile. He could tell she was trying to make

light of the situation, and redirect the conversation when she said, "And you accuse me of being the stubborn one."

"I'm serious. What about your friends?"

She sucked in a breath and let it out very slowly. "Luke—"

"I want to know."

"It's nothing. It's just that I don't have any. Not really."

Okay, that took him by surprise. Although, now that he thought about it, it shouldn't have shocked him. He'd spent an entire week with her and had yet to see her take any calls or texts, or get together with any girlfriends after work.

"What are you talking about?" he asked.

"I just...I don't have friends."

"I don't get that. You're smart, funny, kind and beautiful. What's not to like?"

What's not to like indeed.

"You don't have to say things like that." She stared at her lap, and the vulnerability he saw in her—an emotion she hid so well—hit him harder than a blast of C-4. "Not to me."

"Jesus, are you serious?" He shook his head, hardly able to believe what he was hearing. It brought out the protector in him and he hugged her tighter, but she shrugged like it was nothing.

"It's okay. I get how things work. I learned early on not to have any expectations of people." Her eyes met his, and a rush of tenderness moved through him. "People use me for one thing or another and then move on. It's fine. Really."

Like fuck it was fine.

His gut clenched because as she continued to look deep into his eyes, it suddenly occurred to him that she'd lumped him in with everyone else. And why wouldn't she? Really, when it came right down to it, he was no different than anyone. He had no intentions of forging anything deeper with her and planned to leave when the job was over. She expected that, and had blatantly told him so.

When he stayed quiet, she went on to explain. "When I was young, kids avoided me because of my brother, but then when they found out I was a Taylor, from Taylor's Market they befriended me, but only because they wanted something from me."

He worked to talk around the lump in his throat. "Is that why you dropped that from your last name?"

"Partly."

Luke's heart thumped and all he wanted to do was take her into his arms, make sweet love to her all night long and show her she was important...to him. It occurred to him that in some ways she was as damaged as he was. Which made him wonder if she hired him because his past didn't matter to her, that she believed *in* him, that she gave second chances.

Because she wasn't like her father.

Footsteps on the dock caught Luke's attention and he spun to see Matt coming his way.

"So you got my messages after all," Matt said, then stopped in his tracks. "Oh, shit, sorry. I didn't realize you had company."

Luke stood and helped Emery up. She brushed her hands over her shorts, and twirled her wine glass in her hand.

Luke shot Matt a hard glance. "And I didn't realize you were all going to be here this weekend."

"Check your phone once in a while why don't you. I've been leaving messages for you to meet us here."

Shit. He'd left it in the truck when they arrived.

Matt gave him a knowing grin. "But I can see you had better things to do with your hands than check your phone." He winked. "I would have turned mine off too."

When Matt's glance left him and went to Emery, Luke felt a flash of possessiveness. He pulled her closer, and said, "This is Emery."

"Hey, Emery. I'm Matt."

"Nice to meet you, Matt," she said. "I've heard all about you."

"I've heard about you too."

That seemed to surprise her. "Really?"

Chatter followed behind Matt and Luke looked up to see Tallulah, Sky and a girl he didn't recognize walking toward the dock.

Sky ran forward and jumped onto Matt's back, just like she used to do when they were kids, and Matt grabbed her legs to give her a piggyback ride.

"Hey, Luke," she called out over his shoulder, then her glance went to Emery. In a reaction much like Matt's, she said, "Oh I didn't realize you were bringing someone."

He introduced Emery, and in turn Tallulah introduced her friend to them.

"This is my friend Kat Stiller from back home," Tallulah said. "She came in with my parents for a visit." She gave Kat a hug. "I'm so happy to have her here." She nudged Matt. "Maybe we can convince her to stay."

"Where's Lexi?" Luke asked. It was rare to see Garrett and Tallulah without their little girl.

"The folks wanted her all to themselves so we thought we'd sneak away for a little adult time." She winked at Matt. "Seems like you beat us to it."

Emery shifted, and sensing she was uncomfortable he came to her rescue and said, "We should probably get going."

Sky gave him a confused look. "What are you talking about, you two aren't going anywhere. Caleb's getting the fire going, and the beer is chilling." She jumped off Matt's back and grabbed Emery's hand. "Come on and help us unpack." She shot a glance over her shoulder and added, "And I have all kinds of childhood stories about Luke to share with you."

"Sky," Luke warned, but it was too late, Emery had been whisked away from him. As he watched her go, his stomach tightened. He was worried that she wouldn't be comfortable around his group of friends. Then he thought about what she'd told him, about having no friends. It made him *want* to share his with her. To bring her deeper into his world.

Oh boy…

"Lucy, you got some 'splainin' to do," Matt began, and put his hand on Luke's shoulder. "Is this the girl that had you all mopey the other day?"

"Matt…" he warned.

"Well you don't look so mopey anymore. In fact, you look downright smitten."

"Mopey? Smitten? 'Splainin' to do? Jesus, Matt, I told you, you've been hanging out with your grandmother too much." Turning the subject around, Luke gestured with a nod to the girls. "And speaking of smitten. When are you going to ask Sky out anyway?"

The grin fell from Matt's face. "We're just friends. And I think Tallulah is trying to hook me up with Kat."

"She's cute, in a *she'll eat you alive* kind of way."

"Yeah. I met her at the wedding last year, but I just wasn't in the mood, you know."

"Believe me, I do know." Oh, yeah, he knew. Luke threw his arm around his buddy. "Let's go drink some beer."

Matt grinned, and put his arm around Luke. "Now that's the best thing I've heard you say all night."

They walked along the dock and back up the cottage, neither one discussing the girls who were getting under their skin, and when he spotted Emery chatting easily with the others, a big smile on her face, his heart tightened. Jesus, he hated the thought of her having no friends, of everyone in her life using her for one thing or another.

The girls disappeared inside and Luke and Matt plunked themselves down by the fire. Garrett reached into a cooler and pulled out two beers. "Where were you?" he asked Luke. "Down by the water playing in the sand?"

Luke shook his head, but the shit-eating grin on Garrett's face was contagious and he found himself grinning right along with him. He scrubbed his hand over his jaw, grabbed the beer Garrett was holding out for him and said, "You're an asshole, you know that right?"

Garrett laughed. "And that would be one of the nicer things people have called me."

Luke twisted the cap off and took a long pull from the bottle. "Be nice to her."

"Hey, I'm always nice."

"Me too," Josh said.

Luke pointed the tip of his beer bottle at Josh. "You," he began, "can stay away from her."

"Stay away from who?" Sky asked as she came out and plunked herself down on the arm of Matt's Adirondack chair.

Instead of answering Matt handed her his beer and she took a drink and passed it back. As Luke watched it occurred to him that the two had no idea how intimate they were with one another. The rest of the girls came out and sat around the fire as Caleb got it blazing.

Emery sat next to him and, unable to help himself, he reached for her hand. Sexual chemistry bubbled between them and he wondered if the others could feel it.

He squeezed his fingers around hers, and in no time at all they were all kicking back and enjoying themselves, that is until Sky started telling Emery stories of his childhood antics.

When he saw Emery laugh—at his expense—he buried his face in his hands. She pulled them away, gave him an amused look, and then, without warning, she dropped a soft kiss onto his mouth. As if she realized what she'd done, she looked away sheepishly. He caught Garrett's raised eyebrow, and was pretty sure he was going to have to beat the crap out of him before the night was over.

By the time the fire had died down, they'd all put back way too much beer. Garrett was the first to call it a night. A mischievous look danced in his eyes as he grabbed his wife. "Dibs on the king-sized bed," he said as Tallulah snuggled in close.

"That's my bed," Caleb announced, jabbing his thumb into his chest.

"Caleb, remember that time in Afghanistan—"

"Fine," Caleb said, cutting him off. "I'll sleep on the boat." He pointed to Garrett. "Then we're even."

"Nah, it's going to take a lot more than that to get us even."

Caleb shook his head. "What was that Luke said about you being an asshole?"

They all laughed, and Luke looked at Emery, loving the way she was sitting back and enjoying the easy camaraderie between friends. It was easy to see she was soaking it up, and how much she longed to be a part of a group of friends like this.

"Yeah, I'll join you," Matt said to Caleb, like he was making it perfectly clear that he wouldn't be shacking up with Kat, who actually seemed more interested in Josh anyway.

Luke stood and pulled Emery up with him. "Ready to call it a night?" he said as he brushed her hair from her face. She yawned and he smiled. "I'll take that as a yes."

"It's been a long week."

"And hard," he whispered. "Don't forget hard."

She just shook her head at his one-track mind.

They followed the others inside, and took the stairs to the loft—the spot they had claimed for themselves last night and woke up together in this morning—as everyone found a spot to sleep. Matt and Caleb went to the boat, while Garrett and

Tallulah took the big room. Kat and Sky claimed the other smaller beds while Josh found himself on the sofa in the main room.

"No privacy tonight," Luke said as he glanced at the bed they'd made wild love in last night. He brushed his thumb over her bottom lip. "You could probably use a break anyway," he teased.

She smiled at him, but he sensed a shift in her. "Everything okay?"

Her hair fell over her shoulders when she nodded, but suddenly everything felt different between them. His heart raced as foreign emotions ambushed him. It was obvious something was happening, something he had no control over.

The place fell quiet and their eyes met as they peeled off their smoky clothes, leaving them on the floor. Emery reached into her bag and pulled on a T-shirt. He stood there looking at her, trying to remember how to breathe as she climbed beneath the sheets. As it grew harder and harder to fill his lungs, Luke stripped naked and settled in next to her. He reached for her hand and their fingers linked, like they needed the contact. They lay there for a moment, electricity crackling between them as they stared at the star-studded night through the skylight, both lost in their own thoughts.

After a while Luke rolled to his side, her nearness making him breathless and his need for her too strong to deny. "Hey," he whispered, not wanting to disturb the others. "You awake?"

"I'm awake," she said quietly, turning to face him.

Her scent wrapped around him and he knew he was done for. He put his hand around her head and drew her to him, desperate, so goddamn desperate to take her again. His mouth found hers and he kissed her gently, softly, running his tongue over her lips slowly so he could savor her in her entirety. She moved beside him, her body so warm and welcoming, so responsive to his touch, it did the strangest things to him.

"God, you taste good," he whispered into her mouth, the hunger he felt for her consuming him.

In the warmth of the loft, the moonlight slanted in through the skylight and fell over their bodies. It created such a cozy, romantic atmosphere, and had him wanting to lose himself in her again. It was impossible to ignore the heat between them. The blankets ruffled as he pulled her beneath him, her small gasp letting him know he'd taken her by surprise.

"Emery," he whispered into her ear, feeling a strange new pull between them as she relaxed beneath his body. Even though Josh was just below them, and they probably shouldn't have been having sex with so many within earshot, he murmured, "I need to be inside you, sunshine."

"We're in a loft," she whispered and pointed toward the main level. "And Josh is right there."

"I know," he said, but goddammit he needed her in the worst way. "You're just going to have to try to be quiet this time."

That pulled a smile from her. She opened her mouth to counter, and he brushed his lips over hers. She melted into his touch and he lifted his head to see her face as he pushed her hair from her forehead. The moonlight fell over her, and as she gazed up at him with those expressive eyes of hers, it made him think about all her hurts. His heart thumped harder, everything inside him reaching out to her, and wanting to take away past pain.

Emotions passed over her eyes as their gazes met and locked, the look so potent, so compelling, it touched something deep inside him. She lightly ran her hands over his back, her fingers caressing gently. This time there was no pulling and pushing, just a soft exploration as she reacquainted herself with his body.

He reached between their bodies and pushed her T-shirt up. Working to keep his breathing regulated and silence his groans of want, he kissed the outer edge of her breast and her body came alive beneath him. She moved against his mouth, and as her body writhed with want, the bed coils squeaked beneath them.

"Shit," he murmured, and when she giggled, Luke put his hand over her mouth, which made them both laugh a little louder.

"I feel like I'm back in high school doing something I shouldn't be doing," he whispered into her ear.

"It does feel kind of inappropriate doesn't it," she responded. "Not that I did this kind of thing in high school."

"Well then, that makes me want to do it all the more. Everyone should have naughty high school memories."

"You're a bad influence, Luke Phillips."

"I know."

His mouth found hers again, and he kissed her deeply, everything in what they were doing suddenly feeling far more intimate than ever before. His blood pounded hard as he licked a path down her flesh. He swiped his tongue over her belly button, then settled between her legs. She opened for him, and it was crazy how much he wanted to pleasure her, to plant himself between her thighs all night and make her come until sun up.

He licked her lightly and her hips came off the bed. Warmth streaked through him as she responded. Jesus, he'd never tire of tasting her. He touched her thighs to widen them, and his fingers began a slow climb. When he reached her hot core, he pushed two fingers inside and her liquid heat lubricated his hand. Fuck. He loved how she was always so hot and ready for him.

His cock throbbed as he pushed his fingers into her, slowly circling the bundle of nerves he now knew so well. Her hands raced over his shoulders, and for some reason this time her touch felt different. Entirely lost in the moment, in her, his body began thrumming, wanting to be inside her, but wanting more to pleasure her.

She made a whimpering noise, and gripped the bedsheets. He grinned up at her, watching her struggle to be quiet. She was so adorable and his depth of desire for her was pretty damn frightening. He swiped her clit, knowing just how she liked it, and her pussy muscles spasmed and drew his fingers in deeper. He bit back a curse. Christ, he loved the way she came for him. If he had it his way, he'd spend the rest of his life in bed with her, just making her come over and over again.

When her muscles stopped quivering, he climbed over her and pulled on a condom. His mouth found hers as he pushed in slowly, taking his time to concentrate on each point of pleasure as he gave her inch by inch.

Her body softened, opened and he gave her all of himself, burying himself in her balls deep. The second he entered her, a new, deeper intimacy formed between them, a connection like he'd never felt with another woman. He never knew it could be like this. Not like this.

He stayed still, having no desire to move or ever leave this bed, this position. Yeah, burying himself in her like this forever sounded like a pretty damn good idea.

"Luke," she whispered breathlessly. "Please..."

He had no idea what she was pleading for, he only knew that whatever it was, he needed it too. With slow, easy strokes, he moved his hips, his cock sliding in and out of her. He briefly pinched his eyes shut and took his time to feel everything as he made love to her.

Flames moved through him and his breath grew shallow.

He went up on one elbow and looked at her, took in the warmth in her eyes, the expression on her face. He'd always wanted her, but tonight it felt different. He took a deep breath, rattled by the emotions she brought out in him. Her eyes darkened as she came, and he kissed her, burying her muffled cries as he joined her in orgasm. After a long while he pulled back, and as her lashes fluttered up at him, he knew he hadn't just crossed a line in the sand with her. He'd jumped on it, mocked it, and kicked it to the curb as he took what he wanted...no...needed.

Ah, Jesus. He was in so much fucking trouble.

10

Emery glanced up from her chair and couldn't help but smile when she found Luke standing in her doorway. "Hey," she said, her mind going back to the glorious weekend they'd just had, to when she opened herself up to him emotionally as well as physically. Her heart raced, and even though she was used to people taking and then leaving, as she looked at him now, she knew there was something deeper between them, could feel it in every fiber of her being. They'd connected on another, more meaningful level, and for the first time in her life, she felt important, cherished, like she truly meant something to someone. Then there were his friends. They'd been so kind, and contrary to what Luke had said, she actually felt like she fit into his world. The only things his friends had wanted, were to ensure she was comfortable and had a good time.

"Hey yourself." He stepped in, and dropped a soft kiss onto her mouth. "I have to take off. I'm meeting a guy about a van, and then I want to stop by the pawnshop."

"Okay," she said, thinking about the private errand she wanted to run.

He gave her a wink. "Maybe when I get back we can cut out early."

"I think I'd like that," she said, and then he gave her another kiss before he stepped back into the market.

As soon as he left, Emery grabbed her purse and slipped out the back, not wanting Colt or Tanner to see where she was going. She walked quietly through the back streets, then hailed a cab. Ten minutes later, she sat in the backseat and stared up at the building where she'd seen Luke's sister a few days ago.

Feeling a bit nervous, and knowing full well she was over-stepping boundaries, she waited a bit longer. She knew it was a long shot coming here in the hopes of seeing Allison. His sister was likely already up and gone for the day. Emery was about to climb from the cab and try knocking on her door anyway, when up ahead at the corner, she spotted Allison coming from the coffee shop.

"Wait here," she said to the driver.

With her stomach in knots, she slipped from the backseat and walked toward her. Allison had ear buds in and seemed lost in her thoughts as she walked toward Emery.

Just as she stepped past her, Emery called out to her. "Allison," she said loud enough to be heard over the music.

Allison spun around and pulled her ear buds out. Her eyes narrowed as if she were trying to place Emery.

Emery held her hand out. "Hi, I'm—"

Just then Allison's eyes went wide and she took a distancing step back. "I know who you are."

Okay, that took Emery by surprise. "You do?"

"Of course. How could I ever forget a Taylor, considering your father was responsible for ruining my family?"

As anger radiated off Allison, Emery's entire body stiffened, and her voice lodged in her throat. Oh God, maybe she was making a big mistake here. She took a small step back.

"I'm sorry. I shouldn't have come."

"Why did you come?" Allison asked, staring at her with those same haunted gray eyes she'd become so familiar with.

Emery wrung her fingers together. "I wanted to talk to you about Luke."

A bevy of emotions moved over Allison's eyes. "What about him?"

"I think he'd really like to see you."

Allison went quiet for a very long time, her emotions so close to the surface, then she finally asked, "Did he say that?"

"Not in so many words. But I think he's afraid to talk to you. He's afraid you hate him."

Emery's heart went out to Allison as tears welled up in the girl's eyes. Her shoulders sagged, and her backpack slipped off and fell to the ground. "I don't hate him. How could I ever hate him? He's my brother."

"I know where he is if you want to see him."

Her brow furrowed, but a mixture of worry and love danced in her eyes. "You do?"

She nodded. "He's probably going to kill me for doing this, but he's hurting, Allison, and I don't want him to hurt anymore."

"Why do you care?"

Because...she loved him.

"He's working for me."

Allison's head came up with a start, her long dark ponytail bouncing around her shoulders. "He's what?"

"He's setting up a security system at my market."

"Oh my God." Allison gave a low, slow whistle. "I never thought he'd step foot in that place again." She looked at the ground like she was reliving painful memories. "Something really important must have driven him to do it, otherwise..."

Emery took a moment to think about that. There was no

denying that she had spent time wondering why he'd taken the job after all he'd been through with her father.

"If you can go see him, I think you should." Allison didn't say anything, she just stared at Emery, her eyes glassy. Emery got the sense that Allison's thoughts were so far away, she was looking through Emery, not at her. Even though she was over-stepping boundaries, Emery couldn't help but ask, "Why did he push you out of his life?"

She gave a slow shake of her head. "I don't know. Juvie changed him I guess." She went quiet and the ghosts returned to her eyes. "He was such a great brother and a great guy. Everyone loved him. Then he got hard, hateful, especially toward me." Pain moved over her face, and Emery's eyes filled with tears as she thought about how tough life must have been after Luke had been removed from her life, for all of them. "I believed in him, you know. I knew he didn't steal anything. Even though he swore to me he did, and told me I was better off without a thief like him in my life." She tugged on her ponytail. "His best friend Shane supported him too. He used to justify Luke's actions by saying desperate times make people do desperate things. But my father turned his back on him. It destroyed our family."

Emery thought back to Trent, and how desperate times drove him to steal for his family. "Maybe he stole to help feed his family."

Allison gave her an odd look. "I'm guessing you know my brother pretty well if you're here talking to me."

"I do." Or at least she thought she did.

"Well, if you did you wouldn't be asking me that question."

Emery's heart raced. *What the heck?* She wanted to ask what Allison meant by that, to get to the bottom of matters, but before she could get her thoughts organized enough to ask, Allison's friend called out to her. "Hey, Allison."

Allison looked at Emery, then at her friend. She picked her backpack up from the ground and tossed it over her shoulder. "I have to go."

"Will you go see Luke?"

"All I've ever wanted to do was go see my big brother. He was the one who pushed me away."

"Here." Emery grabbed a piece of paper from her purse and scribbled his address down. "I understand if you don't want to come by the market. He can also be found here."

Allison took it and after she left, Emery's thoughts ran a million miles an hour. Her legs felt numb beneath her as she went back to the cab. She stared out the window and tried to make sense of her conversation with Allison. She thought she knew Luke, having spent so much time with him lately, bonding with him on another level, but after talking to Allison, she was wondering if she really knew him at all.

A short while later, she slipped in through the back door of the market. She booted up her computer, looking for information on Luke, and what had actually happened all those years ago. Shuffling noises at her door had her lifting her head.

"Dad," she said, climbing to her feet to give him a hug.

"Where you been, missy?" he asked, and when she looked at him, she noticed the new lines around his eyes. He looked so tired, so worn out, like he hadn't slept in days.

"I was away with some friends," she said, not wanting to upset him.

He scoffed. "Friends? You don't have any friends."

Her stomach clenched and she inched away, hating that he would say that to her. She loved her dad dearly but he could be so hard sometimes.

"You were with that guy, weren't you?"

"I was just at a cottage."

He scowled. "Yeah with him." He raised his cane. "If you

know what's good for you, you'll stay as far away from him as possible." He gave her a disapproving stare. "Once a thief always a thief."

Her father could say what he wanted about her, but she was not going to stand there and let him disrespect Luke. "I don't think—"

He tapped his head and cut her off. "Then maybe you should think."

"What are you talking about?"

"Why do you think he took this job?"

"Because I hired him and he needed the work." At least that's the only logical reason she could come up with.

"No. He took it because it was his way to get back at me. He's probably robbing you blind as we speak."

Something really important must have driven him to do it...

As Allison's words pinged around inside her brain she stared at her father. "Dad—"

"You'll see, Emery. You'll see," he said, and he pounded his cane on the floor and walked out of her office.

With her stomach in turmoil, she walked back into the market and restocked shelves. As the end of the day approached, she made her way back to her office, to return to her search, trying to find out more about Luke, and the court records. Lost in her search, she hadn't heard him approach.

"Sorry it took me so long," he said. "I couldn't make it back any earlier."

She glanced up then quickly shut her laptop as he dropped a kiss onto her mouth. Trying to appear casual, she asked, "How did you make out with the van?"

He gave her an odd look, glanced at her closed computer, and sat in the chair across from her. "Good. He was a tough negotiator, but I got a fair deal. We'll be signing the papers tomorrow."

Just then her assistant Tami poked her head in the door. "You busy?"

"No, come in," Emery said, waving her in.

"I just cashed everyone out, and here's five thousand." Tami handed over a roll of bills. "There's enough in the tills for morning." She gave them both a smile and said, "I'm clocking out." She looked at Luke. "Will I be seeing you tomorrow or are you guys all finished?"

"Everything should be in place by tomorrow."

"Well I'll see you tomorrow then."

After she left, Emery stood, opened her safe and placed the money inside. She turned back to Luke. "And the pawn-shop. Did you find anything out?"

He opened his mouth like he was about to say something, then he shut it again. "No, nothing." He wiped his hands on his jeans, and avoided her eyes. In that instant she sensed he was hiding something from her. "Oh, and I have some things to take care of tonight, so I won't be around."

"Oh, okay," she said, her heart racing from this unex-pected turn of events. What was going on? Was he pulling away? Good God, maybe she really didn't know him at all. And maybe he was backing off because he was almost finished with the job, which meant he was finished with her.

Old doubts resurfaced and her stomach cramped, some small part of her brain reminding her that people used her and discarded her when they'd gotten what they wanted.

Was she wrong to think Luke was different?

———

Luke took a long pull from his bottle as he kicked back at Sky Bar. He'd told Emery he couldn't see her tonight because he had some personal things to take care of. He didn't miss the curious yet almost dejected way she'd looked at him, like now that the job was almost over he was tossing her away like she was yesterday's news. After learning about her past, he knew she expected that from him. But how in the hell could he climb into her bed and make sweet love to her when he was holding back such important information? It just didn't feel right.

He turned to Garrett. "What the fuck am I supposed to do?"

"You're going to have to tell her."

"How can I do that? It will crush her."

"Then maybe you can talk to Taylor. Put the fear of God in to him and maybe he'll never do it again."

"What kind of fucking man does that to his daughter?"

"Believe me, in my job I see lots of fucked-up shit."

He thought about that for a moment. "Do you think you can do me a favor?"

"Sure."

"Can you do a little digging on Taylor? Find out what he's up to and why he's stealing. He must need the money for something."

"I'll see what I can do."

Luke pushed his beer aside, and needing time to sort through things, he stepped away from the bar. "I need some air."

He jumped on his bike, and drove around town. Soon enough he found himself outside the market. He sat on his bike and watched Emery move around inside. His heart raced and it damn near killed him not to go to her, but he didn't know how to face her when he was holding such hurtful information. He spotted someone in the store with her. He narrowed his eyes, his protective instincts going on high alert. A moment later the door opened, and she walked out with Trent trailing behind her.

What the hell was Trent doing there?

Emery went one way down the street toward her town-house and Trent went the other, cutting the corner and heading to the seedier part of town. Luke followed him, and when he caught up to him on the sidewalk, Trent turned to him, surprise in his eyes.

Luke shut down his bike. "Hey, Captain America, what are you doing in this neck of the woods?"

Trent kicked a rock, and said, "Working."

"Oh, yeah, working for who?"

He nodded behind him. "Emery."

"She hired you?"

"Yeah. I actually asked for a job." He looked down, shuffled slightly, then looked back up at Luke. "And well, I wanted to talk to you, to say thanks."

"Thanks for what?"

Trent gave him a look like he was dense. "You know. For hooking me up at the center." A small smile tugged at his mouth. "I actually really like it there. And...well...I wanted to say thanks for sending the food to my house. My brother really loved all the licorice. I told Emery I wanted to work off the debt."

That's why she'd taken down his address. His heart pinched and he could feel himself falling deeper and deeper in love with her.

Emery, sweet Emery, who'd given him so much of herself.

"Okay, Trent. Go home. I'll see you at work tomorrow."

"G'night."

Luke started up his bike and made his way back down the street. As he passed the market he caught a light on in the back. He peered in and an uneasy feeling curled around him. Had Emery come back, or was someone else in her store? Luke took off down the street and made his way to Tanner's place, to where his van was parked outside. He hopped off his bike, and fished his keys from his pocket. Sliding the side door open, he pulled a chair up in front of the monitors and turned on the live feed. Without a camera in Emery's office he couldn't tell if it was her in there or not, but when her father stepped back into the market, quietly closing the office door behind him, Luke's throat tightened. Taylor moved toward the back door, and the video showed him shoving a bundle of money into his pocket, the same bundle he'd watched Emery lock up earlier that day.

Oh, Jesus, this was so bad. Her own father, the man who'd put Luke away for stealing, was robbing the place blind, and had no idea Luke was capturing it all. *Son of a bitch!*

With a pit in his stomach the size of a tennis ball, Luke made his way back home. Emery had so many people counting on her and she needed that money. But because she kept the state of the business private, not wanting to upset her father, he likely didn't know how bad things really were, how hard this would be on her bottom line.

He grabbed Rex and took him out for a run to help clear his head, but his mind was still racing by the time he fell into bed, into a fitful sleep. Come morning, he made his way to the shower, hoping a splash of cold water would clear his sleep-deprived brain. The pinging of his cell drew his attention. He glanced at it, and saw a message from Garrett. It said one word and one word only.

Gambling.

Shit.

Clearly Taylor must have lost a bundle gambling, and desperate times caused people to do desperate things, but this was just damn wrong.

He raked his hands though his hair, trying to figure out what he was going to do about the situation. He couldn't let him do this to his daughter, yet he didn't have it in him to break Emery's heart. Turning the water to cool, he jumped into the shower and as he waited for it to wake him up, his mind sorted through matters. What the hell was he going to do? There was no denying that he'd fallen for Emery. She was sweet, sexy, different from any woman he'd ever known. Even though they came from different worlds, she fit in so nicely with his friends, and he wanted to share his circle with her, wanted her to feel like she belonged, especially after she'd shared her hurtful past with him. He thought back to when she'd first hired him. He couldn't help but think she did it because she believed in him.

His heart squeezed as he considered that longer, and the solution to his problem finally came to him. As he warmed to the idea, he shut the water off, and put a plan into motion.

He dressed quickly and made his way outside. Thirty minutes later, he pulled his bike up behind the van, parked it and climbed off. He slid the door open and stuck his head inside.

"Morning," he said, but when he caught the strange look on his comrades' faces he shot a glance toward the monitors to find Taylor talking to Ethan Lane—who was carrying a bouquet of flowers—as they walked toward Emery's office. A wave of possessiveness moved through him, and he drew a slow breath to calm himself.

Instead of reacting, he put on his best professional face and said, "We just have a few last-minute things to do, then we're done." He looked at Colt. "You've gone over everything with Emery that I told you to?"

"Yup," he said.

He looked at Tanner. "The alarm system has been integrated with the phone lines?"

"Finished setting it up a few minutes ago. The system is good to go."

"Okay, just a few more things I need to test and then we're out of here."

Luke made his way back into the store, just as Lane was leaving Emery's office. It took everything he had not to punch the guy in the throat and tell him to stay the fuck away from Emery. But that would have to wait. Right now he was on a mission.

He walked along the perimeter of the store, looking over the equipment he installed as he waited for the opportune moment. In order for him to do what needed to be done, he needed Emery and her father out of the office. Then he'd be having a one-on-one with Taylor himself.

He hung around, double and triple checking the system and basically just wasting time as he waited. He walked past the deli, and when he heard her father raising his voice his body tensed and he moved toward the office.

"I told you he was no good," Taylor said. "Ethan Lane is the kind of man you should be with. Not one who'd steal five thousand dollars from you to get back at me."

"Dad—" The anxiety Luke heard in her voice twisted his gut.

"Why the hell did you hire him anyways?"

"He was the only option. I was desperate and his company was the only one who could do it on such short notice."

Jesus...

"And I'm guessing you opened the safe in front of him a time or two?"

"Yes, but—"

Luke took a measured step closer, his stomach twisting as he eavesdropped.

"No buts about it," her father said. "He's behind all this. He used you to get to me, Emery."

Emery spotted Luke near the doorway. When her eyes

met his and he spotted confliction, doubt brewing just below the surface, the bottom dropped out of his world.

She didn't trust him.

"Well speak of the devil," her father said, lifting his cane. "You better get your ass out of here before I call the cops on you again and get you locked up."

He glared at Taylor and fisted his hands at his sides as anger moved through him. After a long while he turned his focus to the woman he loved, a woman who he thought believed in him.

"Emery," he said, needing so much from her.

"I...I..." Her glance bobbed back and forth between Luke and her father. In a show of allegiance, her father stepped closer to her and put his arm around her.

While he wanted to tell her the truth, he knew he couldn't do it. Couldn't come between a father and his daughter. Not then, and not now. He pulled the money from his back pocket and slapped it on the table. "Here you go."

Emery's face paled. "Luke?" she asked, her voice as shaky as her hands.

"It's all there," he said. He cast a hard glare at her father. "And just so you know, I'm giving you something you never gave me."

"Oh yeah, what's that, boy?"

"I think you know."

Luke glared at him, a deadly warning written all over him as he gave the old man a moment to digest his words.

When Taylor's face fell, they exchanged a look of understanding—one that said Taylor knew Luke was fully aware that Taylor had taken the money and he'd have hell to pay if he didn't get his shit together and make it right with his daughter.

With that he cast Emery one last look, his heart splintering into a million tiny pieces.

"Maybe your old man is right about Lane too," he said, then he walked out of the market and her life, forever.

———

Emery watched him go, hardly able to believe what was happening. Tears filled her eyes and she felt physically ill. She clutched her stomach as bile punched into her throat.

How could this be happening? She'd shared so much with Luke, thought she knew him. This really didn't seem like something he would do, but how could she dispute the facts, or contradict the evidence her father had put right in front of her?

"How the hell did he come up with that kind of money?" her father whispered under his breath.

"What?" Emery asked, spinning to face him. "What did you just say?"

Color moved into her father's face and his cloudy eyes widened. "What? Nothing," he said. "It was nothing."

"No, it wasn't nothing. If he stole the money, like you said, then why are you so surprised that he 'came up with that kind of money'?"

"I...I...just... Emery, the man is no good. Stay away from him. Ethan is the man you should be with. Luke even said so."

"I want to know," she said, standing up to her father for the first time in her life. Something was going on here, and she was damn determined to get to the bottom of it. "Why did he say he was giving you something you'd never given him?"

She took a moment to think about it, and suddenly all the pieces known as Luke Phillips began to fall in to place. She'd once heard Luke say he'd never come between a father and a daughter—which undoubtedly was why he pushed his sister away. She also heard him say more than once that he believed in giving second chances.

"Oh my God. You took the money." She took a small step back.

"Emery, it's not like that."

"You took the money," she said again, shaking her head in disbelief.

"I got myself into a bit of trouble, but I'm going to get the money back. I promise."

"You took the money and blamed it on Luke. How could you do that to him, to me?"

"Because I don't like that boy."

"You put him away for stealing, yet how is what you did any better?"

"It's my business, so technically I'm not stealing."

"No, it's my business now. You left it in my hands, and you've been stealing from me. I hired Luke to install a new system because I could barely pay the bills, when all along it was you taking things from here. I kept the state of the business from you to protect you."

"I'm sorry." Her father fell into her chair, looking older than she'd ever seen him. "I'll get some help. I promise. I never meant to hurt you and I didn't know things were going bad. I...I just. I was desperate."

Desperate times make people do desperate things.

She took a moment to think about her conversation with Allison, and how Shane had told her desperation drove a person to do desperate things. She considered the way Shane had reacted when he met her, then thought about his wife Callie, and little girl Amber, who was twelve years old. Twelve years ago, Luke was put in juvie. Her mind raced, thinking about everything Luke had said and done since she met him, especially with Trent.

"What did he steal?" she asked, hysteria lacing her voice. "What did Luke take from this market?"

"That was a long time ago."

"Tell me."

He shrugged, a deep sadness on his face. "Just some food."

"What kind of food?"

He shrugged. "Peanut butter, bread. You know, the usual kid stuff."

Peanut butter...

Oh God!

That's why Allison had asked her how well she knew Luke. Luke had a peanut allergy, and Allison likely did too, which meant Luke hadn't taken the food to feed his family.

I knew he didn't steal anything...

As Allison's words banged around inside her head, everything started to make sense. Shane must have been the one who'd taken the food—to feed his pregnant girlfriend—and Luke had taken the fall. That had to have been what happened and why Shane had stood behind Luke, and was hell bent on giving back to the community and helping the youth.

She shot her father a glance, and watched him sag in his chair. "You sent an innocent boy away and he lost everything because of it." She looked at the money Luke had tossed onto her desk. "And in return he took the blame for this and gave you a chance to make things right with me."

She picked up the bundle of money, money he'd taken from his savings and had planned to use to expand his business and give his comrades work. Her stomach clenched. How could she not have believed him, believed in him?

Luke was a good man, a wonderful, loving guy and she drove him from her life because she second-guessed his integrity.

How could she have been so stupid? She thought he was

pulling back from her because he was through with her, but it was because he knew the truth about her father. He was trying to protect her, and in turn she threw it all in his face.

But why didn't he ever tell her all this? Did he not trust her enough to tell her about his past? Or maybe he kept it to himself because he was too afraid she wouldn't believe him? Either way, even if he no longer wanted her, she somehow had to do right by him, to show him that he was the best man she knew.

$$11$$

"That's all pretty fucked up," Garrett said, before taking a pull from his bottle.

Luke nodded. "Yup."

"So now what? You're just going to sit here and mope about it."

"What the fuck?"

Garrett twirled his bottle. "If I loved her I'd fight for her."

"Did you not hear anything I said? She thought I took the money." He scoffed. "I thought she was different."

"No you didn't." He glared at Garrett. "If you thought she was different, you would have told her about your past, you would have opened up to her, and put your heart on the line. You didn't do that because you didn't expect her to be different than any other rich bastard who screwed you over."

"And in the end she *did* screw me over. She believed her father over me."

"Maybe she's not the one with the problem. Maybe you are. Maybe you set yourself up for failure with her."

"Why would I do that?"

"Because you have a goddamn chip on your shoulder, and

deep down expect the worst from those on the other side of the tracks."

"And I got the worst, didn't I? She didn't believe in me. So what's your point?"

"You set her up for that, Luke."

"How?"

"By not telling her what really happened, now or all those years ago. Jesus, are you really going to risk losing the best thing that ever happened to you because you can't let go of the past?" Garrett placed a hand on Luke's shoulder. "It's tough, but you have to move forward, my man. Believe me, I saw the way she looked at you. She is different. And you're going to have to lay your heart on the line and trust in her enough to believe she isn't going to stomp on it."

Luke pushed away from the bar. "I gotta get out of here." He stepped outside, jumped on his bike and went for a long ride, his mind going over everything that had happened, especially his conversation with Garrett.

Was he right? Had Luke really set himself up for failure? After a long while he made his way back to his place, and when he spotted a female figure near the entrance of his building his heart raced.

He parked, and jogged to the door, but as he approached, his breath caught and his knees nearly went out from underneath him. He sucked in air, but could barely fill his lungs.

"Allison," he whispered. He glanced around. "What...how?"

She looked up at him with those big gray eyes of hers and her voice sounded shaky when she said, "I heard you wanted to see me."

His heart raced, pounded against his chest. "Allison," he said again, pulling her in tight. Her arms wrapped around him, and he nearly sobbed as he buried his face in her hair.

Her body shook and he held her tighter. After a long while he pulled back.

"How did you know where to find me?"

"Emery. She came to see me."

Luke's heart missed a beat. "She did? Why?"

Allison gave him an odd look. "Because she loves you."

Oh, Jesus, he loved her too. He loved her so goddamn much and now he was going to lose her if he didn't fix this.

He held his sister tight, afraid she would run away from him and he'd lose her again too. "Let's go inside." A few minutes later, they were sitting across from each other in his living room. He reached out and grabbed her hand and as he looked into her eyes, he knew he needed to tell her everything, just like he needed to tell Emery the truth. Garrett was right, he had set himself up for failure, never expecting anyone to believe in him. He believed in second chances, so maybe it was time he gave himself one.

They spent the entire night talking, Luke telling her the truth. In turn she told him she knew about the scholarship, knew it had come from him, and she wanted to be a lawyer because she wanted to ensure that what happened to her brother never happened to anyone else again.

As dawn approached, she stood and stretched. "I have to go. I'm working at Smith and Meyers and I don't want to be late."

Luke hugged her and walked her outside, insisting he drive her home. After dropping her off and making plans for dinner later in the week, he knew he had one more stop to make.

He circled his truck back around and made his way to the market, which was just beginning to fill with early morning shoppers.

He parked and climbed from the cab of the truck, and

tried to quiet his racing heart as he entered, not knowing how Emery would receive him.

He walked to her office but found it empty. He made his way through the store, and when he found her juggling a load of watermelons, moving them to the sale rack, everything he felt for her had his heart squeezing to the point of pain. He couldn't lose her. He just couldn't.

"Need a hand with those melons?" he asked.

She spun around so fast, this time the melons fell to the floor.

"Oh, shit."

"Luke," she said breathlessly. He looked back up at her, and she opened her mouth to say something else but he stepped over the watermelon, and put his finger to her lips to cut her off.

"After going to juvie and doing a tour overseas I never thought I'd be afraid of anything ever again. But I was wrong."

"You were?" she asked quietly.

"Yeah, I'm afraid now. Afraid of losing the best thing that has ever happened to me."

She went quiet for a long time, and his stomach turned over, worry gnawing at him. When she finally spoke, she said, "You know, the second I set eyes on you I knew you were a thief and were going to steal from me."

He flinched, her words cutting deep, but he needed to explain, to make this right.

"Emery—"

This time she put her fingers to his lips to silence him. "You stole my heart."

"Emery... I..." he began, not really understanding what she was saying to him but wanting her to know the entire truth, wanting to lay his heart on the line and trust in her.

She gave a slow shake of her head. "I don't want to hear it."

He ran shaking fingers through his hair. "Please, Emery."

"No, you don't have to say anything because I know the truth. I know everything. I came to see you last night. But I found you with Allison. I didn't want to interrupt. You two needed time together."

At the mention of his sister his heart swelled. "Thank you for that." Then he realized what else she'd said. "Why did you come to me?"

"I wanted to apologize for the way I acted. You didn't deserve that from me. And I wanted to tell you that you are the best man I know."

He cupped her face. "And you are the best woman I know. Which is why I should be the one apologizing."

"I don't understand."

He blew a slow breath. "Emery, sweet Emery. You reacted the way you did because I set you up for it. I didn't tell you the truth. I walked around carrying my past like it was a badge of honor. I want to move past it, put it behind me, and move forward with you."

She swiped at her eyes. "Luke..."

"I want you in my life. I don't want to spend another day in my bed without you in it. Please tell me you want that too."

"I've always wanted that." A small smile tugged at the corner of her mouth. "Ever since you helped me juggle my melons."

As his heart soared, he held his arms out to his sides, not caring who in her upscale market heard him, or whether they believed him or in him. All that mattered was what Emery thought. "So you can love a thief?"

"Like I said, Luke, the only thing you ever stole from me was my heart, and I'm hoping you'll trust me with yours."

"There is no one in the world I'd trust more with it, sunshine."

She stepped into his open arms and, despite the crowd, he kissed her with all the passion inside him. "I love you, Emery Vincent-Taylor."

"And I love you, Luke Phillips."

AFTERWORD

Thank you so much for reading, HIS MOMENT TO STEAL, in my Line of Duty series. I hope you enjoyed the story! Be sure to check out the other 6 books in the series. Please keep reading for an excerpt of HIS BEST FRIEND'S GIRL.

- His Obsession Next Door
- His Strings to Pull (Novella)
- His Trouble in Tallulah
- His Taste of Temptation
- His Moment to Steal
- His Best Friend's Girl
- His Reason to Stay

Interested in leaving a review? Please do! Reviews help readers connect with books that work for them. I appreciate all reviews, whether positive or negative.

Happy Reading,
Cathryn

"What I wouldn't give for a piece of that."

Skylar Redmond, owner of Sky Bar in downtown Austin, glanced at Kat Stiller, who was licking her lips and looking at Skylar's best friend like he was a fresh slab of meat and she'd just come off an all-veggie diet.

"You've got a thing for Matt?" Sky asked as she refreshed Kat's strawberry daiquiri and slid it to her from the working side of the bar.

"Yeah. He's so hot." She fanned her hand in front of her pretty face, her big green eyes wide as she admired Matt from afar. "Just look at him. All that muscle, those blue eyes, the hair and those hands. God those hands... I bet he really knows how to use them to get his kink on in the bedroom." Kat sighed and spun on her padded stool to glance around the room, one filled with hot soldiers who frequented Sky Bar on a regular basis. "Too bad he's more interested in that book he's reading than he is in getting laid."

"He's studying for his MCATs," Sky explained, stealing another glace at Matt as he focused intently on the pages in front of him, oblivious to everyone and everything around him as he huddled at the far end of the bar. She looked at the jar of peanut butter beside him. Honest to God, if he didn't start eating properly he was going to get sick. He might be crazy busy seven days a week, switching careers from an army field ambulance technician to a civilian medical doctor, but no man could live off of peanuts alone. She grabbed her iPad and punched in an order that went directly to the kitchen. When Matt wasn't in class, studying, or helping with the training of service dogs, he worked at the bar with her, and every cent he made went toward saving for med school. But as his best friend since childhood, and current boss, she was not going to let him starve.

"You think that's all it is?" Kat asked, crinkling her nose.

Pool balls banged and laughter and ribbing could be heard from a half a dozen or so ex-soldiers standing around the pool table. As Sky listened to the camaraderie among friends, she grabbed a cloth and began wiping down the glassware that Dean had brought from the dish pit out back.

"What do you mean?" Sky asked. "What else would it be?"

"I mean, maybe he's not...you know...into women." She shrugged. "Not that there is anything wrong with that. But it could account for his lack of interest."

Sky nearly burst out laughing. Kat was right, there was nothing wrong with that, but she knew Matt. In their teenage years, he was one the biggest hound dogs she knew. He and their other best friend, Caleb Roth, had to fight the girls off with a stick. Those two bad boys from the wrong side of the tracks had their pick of girls. She would know, since they all hung out in Caleb's basement and she'd accidently walked in on them with their girlfriends a time or two.

"No, you're wrong. He likes his women. Believe me, back in the day he had his fair share." Then again, Sky hadn't seen him with anyone since he returned home from his tour overseas a year ago, and plenty of girls at Sky Bar had tried to get his attention. She could only chalk up his lack of enthusiasm to the important entrance exam he was studying for. Switching careers at this point was no easy task, and everyone knew the MCATs were hard to pass, even when prepared.

Kat took a sip of her drink and toyed with her straw. "Or maybe he's already into someone else."

"Yeah, probably the girl in his anatomy book," Sky said, grinning. "That's the only action he's been getting lately." She placed the polished glass on the rack and reached for another. "Besides, I thought you and Josh Mansfield had a thing."

"Yeah, Josh is great, and we've been having some fun, but...I don't know, maybe I'm looking for something more, you know?"

"More?"

She rounded her shoulder and hugged her belly. "I think my biological clock is ticking. Every time I hold Tallulah's sweet baby girl Lexi, all I can think about is having my own child."

Sky nodded as the kitchen bell sounded behind her. "I know what you mean." She grabbed Matt's sandwich from the serving shelf and slid it down the counter to him.

It hit his textbook with a thud, and his head lifted. He took note of the sandwich, then his glance went to her. He gave her a big smile and Sky just laughed, pointed at his plate and said, "Eat."

She turned back to Kat, who was studying her carefully.

"So if you know what I mean, does that mean you want to be in a serious relationship too?" Kat asked.

"Sure," she said, then closed her mouth, not wanting to admit that she was approaching thirty and the one guy she wanted she couldn't have. But she didn't want to go down that depressing road. Instead she redirected the conversation and asked, "I take it Josh isn't the settling-down kind?"

"No, but Matt sure seems like a forever kind of guy, doesn't he?"

She turned and looked at Matt as he bit into his sandwich. He followed it with a swig of soda, then licked his fingers clean—an action that seemed to have Kat squirming on her stool. Honestly, she'd never thought about Matt in that sense before. He'd just always been Matt to her. Playful, laid-back and easygoing most times, yet serious when he needed to be, like when he was studying.

"Yeah, I guess he could be a forever kind of guy," she said with a shrug.

"You guess?" Kat arched a perfectly manicured brow. "Shouldn't you know? You are best friends, aren't you?"

"Yeah, we are."

Kat gave her a once-over, a sly smirk spreading across her face. "Unless there is something more going on between you two that I don't know about. I mean, you are constantly together and he's always giving you piggyback rides." She planted her elbow on the table and opened her palm toward the ceiling. "Like I said, he's a guy who knows how to get his kink on." She went quiet, thoughtful for a moment, then wagged her index finger back and forth between Sky and Matt. "Is there something I should know? Are you two...you know...getting your kink on?"

Sky nearly laughed again. "Hardly. We're just friends. We go way back." Matt, Caleb, her—the three musketeers. "We're not getting our..." she paused and did air quotes around the words, "...kink on."

Kat wagged her eyebrows. "But you want to, right?"

"No! And for the record I'm not into kink."

"Well I am, and I want the whole package. A good, stable guy who knows how to rock my world in the bedroom."

Sky would settle for the good, stable guy. She'd never had anyone rock her world in the bedroom, and a kind, caring man was more important to her than that. "And you think Matt is that man?"

"You tell me. You're his best friend."

"To be honest, I've never thought about Matt and marriage in the same sentence before." Nor did she ever think about Matt and kink, but for some strange reason now that Kat had planted that idea in her head, she couldn't quite seem to get it out. "I guess I just never pictured him wearing a tux and standing at the altar."

Kat frowned into her drink. "That's because you didn't see him at the wedding last year."

"What happened at the wedding?" Matt was the best man at Jenny and Ving's wedding last summer, and Sky was still upset she had to miss the ceremony. She'd come down with a serious stomach flu and no way would she fly to Mississippi under those circumstances and risk giving her germs to anyone in the bridal party. Jenny had sent her a copy of the video but she'd yet to find the time to watch it.

"He looked so good. Definitely like he *belonged* at the altar. Women were throwing themselves at him, and he was always so kind, polite and gentlemanly when he declined."

As Sky eyed Kat, and took in the gloom on her face, she guessed the girl was talking from her own personal experiences with Matt. "He's different than most guys." Kat twirled her straw around her mouth and angled her head to see him. "He's not a player, at least not anymore. And he was so fiercely protective of Jenny and Ving, making sure they had everything they needed and stayed stress free during the entire time. I just bet he'd be crazy possessive of his woman too, inside the bedroom and out." She gave a wistful sigh and added, "The stories he told at the dinner party were funny yet so sweet, you know? I really think he is the whole package."

Sky couldn't help but smile, because Kat was right. Matt was funny and sweet and extremely protective of those he cared about. With no mother to raise him and an abusive father who continuously told him he'd never amount to anything, Matt was anything but a chip off the old block. In fact, he swore he'd never be anything like his old man. He'd spent many nights sleeping in Caleb's basement when his father went on a rampage. Caleb's parents might not have had much to offer, but they opened their hearts to Matt and gave him whatever they could.

"Kat?" she asked, unable to get Kat's assessment of Matt out of her head.

"Yeah."

"What makes you think Matt is into kink?"

A small, knowing smile curled up her lip. "I have a knack for these things, and believe me, he's the kind of guy who knows how to hold a girl down hard and give it to her good."

Oddly enough, a fine shiver moved through Sky, even though she wasn't into that kind of thing. In an effort to disguise her sudden interest, she pointed to the door when it opened. "Tallulah and Garrett are here."

Kat smiled and waved Tallulah over as her husband, Garrett, made his way to the pool table. Like Sky and Matt, Tallulah and Kat also went way back to childhood. Kat had only recently moved to Austin and started working at the hospital as a physical therapist so the two could be closer—and also because, according to her, the guys were way hotter in Texas.

Garrett joined his comrades as Sky went to work on making Tallulah a daiquiri. Tallulah slid onto the stool next to Kat. "What's up?" she asked. "You two looked like you were in a serious conversation."

Kat twisted on her stool and gestured with a nod toward the end of the bar. "Oh, I was just questioning Matt's sexual preferences."

"His sexual preferences?" Tallulah's dark lashes blinked

rapidly as she rolled her eyes. "Is this because he never paid you a lick of attention at the wedding last year and keeps himself holed up in that corner studying?"

"Can we not talk about Matt and licking in the same sentence?" Kat groaned. "And if you want to know the truth, then yes, it is because of that. No matter how hard I tried, I could not get that man's attention." She frowned. "I'm starting to think I'm losing it."

Sky looked at the flamboyant, gorgeous woman with the long, thick, chestnut hair that never went frizzy in Austin's humid weathers. "Losing it? Hardly. You're gorgeous, Kat. I wish I had..."

Her words fell off as the heavy oak door opened once again and Caleb Roth sauntered in. Sky's body warmed all over when he shot her a panty-dropping smile that traveled all the way to her toes, stopping in a few erogenous areas along the way. Unable to help herself, she let her gaze slide downward to take in his easy gait and the familiar way he kicked out his long legs with the same lazy ease Sky remembered from their youth. When Caleb had joined the army years ago, he left their hometown of Austin a boy, but he came back a man. A hot, sexy man who would never think of her as anything more than the pigtailed tomboy who used to climb trees with him and Matt.

"Ah, Sky..."

"What?" she asked, turning back to her friends as they both looked at her with wide-eyed curiosity. She resumed wiping down the glasses, busying her hands and pretending Caleb's mere presence hadn't thrown her off her game.

Tallulah tapped a manicured finger on the oak bar top. "Don't *what* us."

Sky reached for another glass, avoiding Tallulah's raised eyebrows. "Meaning?"

"Meaning, what the hell was that all about?" Tallulah asked.

"I'll tell you what that's all about," Kat piped in. "Sky here has the hots for Caleb."

Tallulah's brown eyes widened. "Oh my God, it's true, isn't it? When did this happen? Tell me everything."

"What's true?" Amber, Sky's head waitress and good friend, asked as she came back to the counter with her tray in hand.

Sky's mind raced as three sets of eyes stared at her. She could lie, but what was the point? They'd all see through it anyway. "Okay, fine, it's true. I have the hots for Caleb. It started when he returned home from overseas last year. There, I said it. Are you happy?"

"Like hell I'm happy," Amber said, planting one hand on her hip in usual Amber fashion. For a minute Sky thought Amber was upset because *she* wanted Caleb but then her friend's lips quirked and she pointed a finger directly at Mr. Hottie himself as he walked over to talk to Matt. "I'll be happy when you go over there and do something about it."

"No way." Sky grabbed Amber's wrist and lowered her hand as she shot Kat a glance. "You're not the one losing it, Kat. I am." She gave a disgruntled shake of her head. "Honest to God, I swear the only way I can get a guy to look at me is to tie a pork chop around my neck."

Her friends laughed and she couldn't help but laugh along with them, even though it was the sad truth. She hadn't been with a guy in ages, and if things didn't pick up soon, she was going to give up hope and start hoarding cats.

Then again, it wasn't like she'd been putting herself out there. After finishing four years of college, switching from an English degree to a business degree so she could successfully take over her father's bar when he suddenly passed away from a heart attack a few years back, all she did was work. Her mom died during childbirth and it had been just her and her father growing up. They were very close and keeping the bar a success was important to her. Not only because it was his pride and joy and he'd named it after her, but because he'd entrusted her with it. That meant everything to her. Someday down the road she could get her English degree and write the book she always wanted to, but right now she needed to put all her energy into the bar and making it a success.

Her heart ached as she thought more about her late father, who she missed dearly. He was one of a kind: smart, successful...a man who started out working in the dish pit, saving every penny he had until he could buy the bar and make it his own. He was kind, giving and cared a great deal about others, even offering his friends odd jobs when they were down on their luck. Her whole life she knew she wanted to marry a man who was as compassionate as her father.

She stole a quick glance at Caleb as he walked to the pool table and picked up a stick. She suspected he was that man. He'd come from very little and had worked hard to get where he was. Now he was an army doctor working up in the San Antonio clinic, giving back to the community and caring for the sick. He usually traveled to Austin on the weekends to hang out with her and Matt. When the weather was good and everyone could get the time off, they all often took off to his cottage at the lake.

"If you like him, then do something about it," Kat said, like it was just so simple. If only it were. "Wouldn't it be worse if you never tried?"

Sky lowered her voice, not wanting anyone to overhear them, even though no one else was sitting near them at the bar and Matt was at the other end, out of earshot. The last thing she wanted was for Matt to know how much she wanted their other best friend and make him feel like the third wheel, uncomfortable and out of place.

"He doesn't see me as anything more than a friend," Sky said. "And he never will. He still calls me Skywalker. As in Luke Skywalker. You know, like I'm one of the guys."

Tallulah leaned to her side and nudged Kat with her shoulder. "Then make him see you as a girl." She shared a smirk with Kat, like the two had a dirty little secret. "Believe me, if anyone can school you on seduction and teach you how to get a guy to notice you as something more, it's our Kat here."

Kat grinned. "You're not opposed to bending over a lot, are you?"

Sky sucked in a quick breath as her mind envisioned her doing just that. God, how naughty, wicked and...*kinky* that sounded. "You're joking, right?" Sky asked. Both girls knew her well enough to know she wasn't bold, like Kat, and had never come right out and seduced a guy before. But dammit, she was tired of going unnoticed.

"No. You have a great ass and it's time he knew it." Kat slid a napkin across the bar top. "Go over to the pool table and drop this in front of him. When you bend to pick it up, be sure to arch your back and let that little skirt you're wearing ride up." Kat winked. "Then you'll have him right where you want him. And believe me, girlfriend—" she snapped her fingers, "—he'll be hard as that stick he's holding."

Sky laughed along with her friends. While that sounded devious, and getting him hard would be nice, she truly wanted him to like her for more than her "great ass". She wanted what Kat wanted and Tallulah had—a forever kind of guy— because settling down with a family someday sounded just about right. While sex was nice, it wasn't her main priority. Finding the right man to settle down with was.

"Well, are you going to go for it?" Tallulah asked.

Sky let loose a long, slow breath and planted her hands on

the bar top. "So let me get this straight. You want me to go over to the pool table, drop this napkin, and bend over to show off my ass because you think that's what it's going to take to get Caleb to finally notice me as something more than his tomboy friend."

All three girls inched back a bit, a strange look coming over their faces. Kat and Tallulah turned their attention to their drinks and Amber scurried off to attend a table.

"What?" Sky asked, wondering if she'd said something offensive. Then again, that whole scandalous setup was *their* idea, not hers, so she had no clue as to why they were all of a sudden acting aloof.

"Thanks for the sandwich," Matt said from behind her, his mouth near her ear, his warm breath fanning over her skin.

She spun around and when she came face-to-face with her childhood best friend, she knew in an instant he'd overheard their private conversation.

With an almost tortured look on his face, Matt looked down and said, "I...ah...I think you dropped something."

She followed his gaze to the floor to find the napkin lying across her shoes like it was some clandestine clue in a secret, devious plot—which of course it was.

And now Matt knew about it!

ABOUT CATHRYN

New York Times and *USA today* Bestselling author, Cathryn is a wife, mom, sister, daughter, and friend. She loves dogs, sunny weather, anything chocolate (she never says no to a brownie) pizza and red wine. She has two teenagers who keep her busy with their never ending activities, and a husband who is convinced he can turn her into a mixed martial arts fan. Cathryn can never find balance in her life, is always trying to find time to go to the gym, can never keep up with emails, Facebook or Twitter and tries to write page-turning books that her readers will love.

Connect with Cathryn:
Newsletter
https://app.mailerlite.com/webforms/landing/c1f8n1
Twitter: https://twitter.com/writercatfox
Facebook:
https://www.facebook.com/AuthorCathrynFox?ref=hl
Blog: http://cathrynfox.com/blog/
Goodreads:
https://www.goodreads.com/author/show/91799.Cathryn_Fox

Pinterest http://www.pinterest.com/catkalen/

Hands On

Body Contact

Full Exposure

Dossier

Private Reserve

House Rules

Under Pressure

Big Catch

Brazilian Fantasy

Improper Proposal

Boys of Beachville

Good at Being Bad

Igniting the Bad Boy

Bad Girl Therapy

Stone Cliff Series:

Crashing Down

Wasted Summer

Love Lessons

Wrapped Up

Eternal Pleasure Series

Instinctive

Impulsive

Indulgent

Sun Stroked Series

Seaside Seduction

Deep Desire

Private Pleasure

Captured and Claimed Series:

Yours to Take

Yours to Teach

Yours to Keep

Firefighter Heat Series

Fever

Siren

Flash Fire

Playing For Keeps Series

Slow Ride

Wild Ride

Sweet Ride

Breaking the Rules:

Hold Me Down Hard

Pin Me Up Proper

Tie Me Down Tight

Stand Alone Title:

Hands on with the CEO

Torn Between Two Brothers

Holiday Spirit

Unleashed

Knocking on Demon's Door

Web of Desire

* 9 7 8 1 9 2 8 0 5 6 7 5 1 *